"I Have to Have You."

In the flickering firelight Boone's chiseled features were harsh and ruthlessly compelling. He looked like a bronzed pagan god. The message in his boldly hot black gaze was primitive and wild.

Fear pounded through Leslie's arteries as he dragged her into the electric warmth of his arms.

"Boone, don't . . . not now . . . I'm afraid." She was trembling in his fierce embrace.

"You don't need to be. All I'm going to do is make love to you."

ANN MAJOR

has developed a style and written engrossing stories that have won her many admirers. She lives with her husband and three children in Texas, where she not only writes but also manages a business and household.

Dear Reader:

SILHOUETTE DESIRE is an exciting new line of contemporary romances from Silhouette Books. During the past year, many Silhouette readers have written in telling us what other types of stories they'd like to read from Silhouette, and we've kept these comments and suggestions in mind in developing SILHOUETTE DESIRE.

DESIREs feature all of the elements you like to see in a romance, plus a more sensual, provocative story. So if you want to experience all the excitement, passion and joy of falling in love, then SILHOUETTE DESIRE is for you.

I hope you enjoy this book and all the wonderful stories to come from SILHOUETTE DESIRE. I'd appreciate any thoughts you'd like to share with us on new SILHOUETTE DESIRE, and I invite you to write to us at the address below:

Karen Solem
Editor-in-Chief
Silhouette Books
P.O. Box 769
New York, N.Y. 10019

ANN MAJOR
Meant To Be

Silhouette Desire

Published by Silhouette Books New York

America's Publisher of Contemporary Romance

Other Silhouette Books by Ann Major

Wild Lady
A Touch of Fire
Dream Come True

SILHOUETTE BOOKS, a Simon & Schuster Division of
GULF & WESTERN CORPORATION
1230 Avenue of the Americas, New York, N.Y. 10020

ISBN: 0-671-46056-0

First Silhouette Books printing December, 1982

10 9 8 7 6 5 4 3 2 1

America's Publisher of Contemporary Romance

Printed in the U.S.A.

For Ted,
my beloved husband,
whose tender care has taught me
the meaning of love

when one had both a career and a child. She'd always been in such a rush, there just hadn't been time to be Tim's glamorous playmate.

Involuntarily she shivered. Even in her ski suit inside the warming house she was cold. Would she ever get used to the climate after living all her life in Austin, Texas? Had she been rash to accept a job in sales with R.B. Dexter Inc., a company that dealt in real estate and construction?

For eight years she'd been a teacher. By coming to Colorado and accepting such a job, she'd turned her back on everything familiar, on every link with her past. It was, she'd tried to tell herself when she'd been in one of her more positive moods, the beginning of a new life.

Never in all the months since Tim had walked out on her had Leslie felt lonelier than since she'd moved to Colorado two weeks ago. And this very minute she felt even lonelier than usual. Perhaps it was just that everyone else seemed to be with someone except her.

Her thickly lashed green eyes suddenly riveted to the most compelling man they'd ever beheld. The mug of hot chocolate—half-raised to her lips—sloshed into the saucer as, unconsciously, she set the cup down.

He was tall and dark and boldly handsome. His hair was black, as were his eyes. His skin was bronzed as though he spent a lot of time outdoors. A black ski suit with a slashing gold stripe molded his muscular frame.

Some quality made the man stand out from the crowd that buzzed on all sides of him, but Leslie was at a loss to define exactly what it was.

Was it his air of grim ruggedness that set him apart, making him seem more like a mountaineer than one of the brightly clad ski resort people? Or was it only that, in spite of his youthful aura, he was not as young as most of the crowd? There were laugh lines etched beneath his eyes and grooves slashed on either side of his mouth.

Leslie estimated the man's age to be at least ten years older than hers, and she was almost thirty.

A deep frown creased Leslie's brows. Surrounding the man were several teenage girls. One of the girls tossed her bright red hair and laughed up at him. For a moment the harsh lines of his face softened, and he smiled. His dark face was illuminated. Then carelessly he leaned over and whispered something in the girl's ear.

Why, he was old enough to be that child's father! A deep anger burned through Leslie, not justified by the stranger but by the hurt he had reminded her of.

Tim had left her because she made him feel old. When he'd hit forty, he'd suddenly bought himself a sports car. He'd changed his style of dress. And last of all he'd decided he needed a woman to fit his new, more youthful image.

Some people called it mid-life crisis. As Leslie gazed angrily at the compelling man across the room, she wondered if every man in the United States were going through it.

As though he felt her looking at him, the man turned and stared across the crowded room directly into her eyes. For a static moment it seemed that the very air that separated them was charged. A powerful emotion that she did not understand swept through her, stimulating every sense in her body.

He was a stranger, yet she had the oddest feeling that somehow, somewhere, they'd known each other before, and that they had been on the most intimate of terms. Yet they hadn't; she knew she could never have forgotten him.

To her horror she watched his smile fade into anger. He stared back at her fiercely with a look of profound shock carved into his handsome features.

The sounds in the warming house blurred into a loud buzz as a feeling of weakness washed over her. Why did he stare as though he desired her even though he hated her utterly? The savage fire of his gaze made her tremble as though he held her and caressed her.

The man was a stranger! Again she asked herself, Why was he staring at her as though he not only knew her intimately but despised her? His sensual mouth twisted in contempt, and he leaned over and said something to the girls at his side.

Leslie's heart began to pound with alarming intensity. The man, his expression ruthless, was coming toward her!

Grabbing for her fur hat and gloves, Leslie raced clumsily from the room. Her ski boots cut into her ankles and prevented her from really running.

Blind instinct drove her on. Another man, a friend perhaps, seized the stranger's arm and prevented him from following her outside.

Later as she sat on the lift chair, Leslie's thoughts kept returning to the man she'd seen in the warming house. Why had he looked at her so fiercely? Did she remind him of someone? And why had she, a thirty-year-old woman, run from him as though she were no more than a frightened child?

Perhaps when he'd seen her staring at him, he'd been angered. A wood frame house at the end of the lift broke above the tree tops and came into view. Then the stranger was forgotten since she needed all her powers of concentration to get off the lift without falling down.

She made two more runs plus a trip to the warming house before she decided to take the higher lift to the very top of the mountain.

It was late in the afternoon, and the sun had long ago been lost in the dense thickness of clouds. Suddenly Leslie realized how cold she was. Her cheeks were cherry red; her toes and fingers felt numb. As she began skiing, she felt increasingly uncoordinated. From time to time, she would stop and rest and enjoy the view. She could see miles and miles of snow-capped mountains fringed thickly with white-flocked fir and spruce.

She was concentrating so completely on trying to move her ankles correctly so that she could approximate parallel skiing and get out of the beginner's wedge, that she failed to notice the sign which indicated she'd wandered onto an expert slope. Suddenly beneath her the slope seemed to plunge straight down, and the yawning whiteness was pocked with huge moguls! True terror quivered through her. She could never ski down that! Hardly had this thought flicked through her brain, than her skis struck a patch of ice and went skidding out from under her. Groping wildly to regain her balance and failing, she felt herself tumbling down, down like an aqua and white ball, until she was buried in a deep drift of snow less than a foot from a tree.

When she opened her eyes and pushed her goggles from her forehead all was whiteness and silence. Ignoring a cutting pain in her ankle, she began digging through the snow trying to find the way out.

Then the deepest, most masculine of voices sliced through the silence. "Need some help?"

In spite of the instant relief the man's voice produced, irritation at the contempt in his tone trembled through her. Wasn't the answer to his question obvious?

"Yes," she managed in a weak, contrite voice.

Hard arms circled her, and she felt the man's hands roam over her body as he pulled her from the snow bank. Then she was staring into the blackest of eyes. A cold gust of air tousled the lock of raven hair that had escaped from his black knit hat.

"You!" He almost snarled the word, and as he stared down at her, the intensity of his forbidding gaze seemed to devour her. He was the very same man she'd seen in the warming house! The shock of recognition turned her face white and sent a faint tremor of exquisite apprehension racing through her.

Suddenly Leslie was terribly aware that she was alone on the still vastness of the mountain with this savage stranger, and a second tremor that had nothing to do with the zero-degree weather quaked through her. "Do we know each other?" Leslie asked, trying to remain calm.

For a long moment he studied her. His eyes roved the delicate oval of her face, her full parted lips, and downward over her curves revealed by her skintight ski suit. She reddened with embarrassment. Somehow his knowing gaze was too intimate to be that of a stranger.

His features were etched with the deepest bitterness. Then suddenly, to her surprise, the tension drained from his face. He almost smiled. "No, I guess we don't."

"Do I look like someone you . . ."

Harshly his voice cut her off. "I'm sorry if I was rude. It's not your fault. . . ." His powerful anger of a moment before seemed to drain away. "But we have more important things to consider—like how we are going to get you down this mountain."

Leslie nodded.

"What were you trying to do—kill yourself?" he demanded.

"N-no . . ."

"You almost hit that tree," he said, indicating the thick spruce less than one foot away.

"I-I didn't realize . . ."

"This slope isn't easy for me, and I've been skiing all my life. A beginner has no business . . ."

"I made a mistake. . . . I . . ." Her voice trailed off. She felt strangely near tears. She was cold and tired, and this man was impossible.

As though he sensed her utter fatigue, he relented. "All right, I'll ski you down the mountain."

"My ankle hurts. I don't know if I can," she admitted weakly.

"If you can't, I can ski down and bring the ski patrol back up, but that would mean leaving you here alone."

"N-no . . ." Strangely, the thought of him leaving her was not at all welcome.

"I think you can make it," he said more gently as though he sensed her fear of him leaving her. "You're able to stand. If we go down very slowly, you'll be okay."

He was so sure that his confidence was contagious.

"By the way," he asked, "what's your name?"

"Leslie," she murmured, suddenly feeling strangely shy.

"Leslie . . ."

14

His deeply masculine voice seemed to caress her as he said her name. She had the oddest impression that he wanted to fit a different name to her face. In spite of the cold, and the throbbing pain in her ankle, she realized she was drawn to this man as she had been to no other. Not even Tim had attracted her to the extent that she felt his presence in every fiber of her body.

Why? As she stared up into his brooding countenance it occurred to her that he was suffering from some raw hurt just as she was. Though she didn't understand the reasons behind his bitterness, she knew too well what pain was. She understood the pride that made him want to mask his pain from the world.

"I know what we'll do," he said at last. "We'll ski through these trees. On the other side of them is a beginner slope. Just take it slow. I know it's steep, but remember, all you have to do is ski across the mountain, not straight down it. I'll be right behind you, in case you fall again."

Somehow just knowing that he was there made everything easier for Leslie. Once she'd picked her way through the trees, she paused to rest, and he was there beside her. She felt the gentle pressure of his steadying touch at her elbow.

"You've done the hard part," he reassured her. His voice was oddly gentle, like his touch.

"That's good news," she murmured. She sensed that all the anger he'd felt toward her was gone—at least for the moment, and only his desire for her remained.

"I must say, skiing with you certainly improves the view." His warm black eyes that roved carelessly over her were alight with masculine interest.

For a moment his gaze left her breathless. Something

was happening between them. Not only was there an intense awareness one for the other, an inexplicable closeness she felt toward him, but she sensed suddenly a building sexual tension. A tiny voice warned that her emotions were rushing her into something she might not be able to handle.

He towered over her, and she felt very small and feminine. It was a pleasant sensation. She realized suddenly how much she'd missed being close to a man.

Her divorce had shattered her self-image. In retaliation to all Tim's insults, she'd refashioned her appearance. She'd let her brownish blonde hair grow long, and she'd lightened it so that golden streaks gleamed. She'd lost ten pounds so that she was model slim and looked gorgeous in the glamorous clothes she took the time to select and wear. But though she looked glamorous on the outside, she was running scared. She didn't really fit her new image, though of course this man couldn't know that. And in that moment she determined he wouldn't know that. She was tired of being old-fashioned and out of date.

Jauntily she tossed him an inviting smile and allowed her eyes to linger on the hard curve of his sensual mouth. She strangled a sigh of the carnal pleasure that the thought of those lips on hers produced.

It was strange, but his admiring gaze and his compliment had done more to make her feel like an excitingly attractive woman than all her clothes or her new hairdo.

"From here on I'll take you down the easiest slopes on the mountain," he said.

"I-I'm sorry for all the trouble I've caused you," she said softly. "I can probably make it from here by myself."

" 'Probably' isn't good enough. I said I'd ski you down

the mountain, and I meant it." The protective quality in his deep voice made Leslie feel warm and snug all over, and she looked up at him, her emerald eyes shining.

"You ready?" he asked roughly.

In answer she stabbed her poles into the soft snow and headed down the mountain. But she started too quickly and tumbled into the snow.

As his strong, hard hands circled her and lifted her to her feet, he pulled her unresisting against his own body for a long moment. "Well, not quite," she amended shakily, very aware of his arms about her. A tremulous smile curved her lips.

He looked down at her for a long time, his expression assessing. Their lips were so close that their steamy breaths mingled. She felt the corded muscles of his thighs, the flat hardness of his stomach, the broad expanse of his chest as she was pressed against him. And some part of her wanted him to go on holding her forever.

Suddenly he smiled, and a wild joy fluttered through her. It was the first time he'd actually smiled at her. "Take it easy from now on, Leslie," he commanded gently.

Every time she fell, he was there to help her. Once when he picked up her fur hat, he put it back on her head himself. As he tucked the shimmering strands of gold beneath the fur, she reveled in the intimate touch of this stranger.

What was happening to her? Had she been without a man so long that she was starved for one? She was sure that he was aware of her attraction for him; every time she looked at him, his intent, smoldering gaze met her own.

When they reached the bottom of the mountain she

looked up into the dark, handsome face looming before her and said, "I don't know how to thank you. . . . I . . ." She was strangely at a loss for words. "Why, I don't even know your name."

"Boone," came his crisp reply.

"Thank you . . . Boone. . . . I don't know what I would have done . . ."

"Don't mention it." His eyes flicked indolently past her. "Do you have your car here?"

"Why?"

"That's the last bus pulling out over there," he said, pointing over her shoulder.

"Oh . . ." Turning to look in the direction he'd pointed, Leslie's eyes trailed the bright blue bus as it disappeared around a steep curve. A tiny sigh of disappointment was emitted through lips tinged blue from the cold. It was a long long walk back to her condominium.

"Would you like me to drive you home?" There was a sensual quality in his deep voice that warned he was probably offering her more than just a ride.

Leslie lifted her gaze to the warm, black eyes that were fixed on her soft features, and she flushed. "I couldn't ask you . . ."

"You're not." His hand went around her waist, and even through the layers of clothing she felt the strength of his fingers burning against her flesh. "I asked you."

All she had to do was say no. Ignoring the blatant message she read in the heated depths of his black eyes, she answered, "Yes, I do need a ride."

What was she doing? part of her mind screamed, accepting a ride with a strange man, letting him touch her in a familiar fashion, allowing herself to be picked up as though she thought nothing of it. Doubtless he thought nothing of it, and he certainly wasn't going to pass up such a willing female.

But was she willing? For eighteen months she'd scarcely had any contact with men other than at work. The few dates she'd accepted had been total failures. All any of the men had wanted was a quick one-night stand. Not one had asked her for a second date. Now for the first time she found herself attracted to a complete stranger, and the sensation was so intoxicating that she wanted to prolong it.

"I hope you're not in a hurry. I left my after-ski boots in a locker in the warming house," she said.

"So did I," he returned, guiding her toward the ski lodge.

As they walked together Leslie saw that Boone's striking looks caught admiring glances from several young women. But he seemed not to notice. Instead he focused all his attention on her. He helped her remove her skis, and then he carried them along with his own to the ski racks. When he pushed open the heavy double doors and waited for her to step inside the ski lodge, she reveled in the luxury of having a man do things for her. It had been so long, and she hadn't realized how much she'd missed all the little things one took for granted in a man–woman relationship.

He escorted her to her locker and told her he'd go on to his and then return.

Leslie snapped the second buckle on her boot, and pain shot through a numbed finger. "Ouch . . ."

Instantly a large warm brown hand covered her injured hand. A tingling thrill leaped through her as Boone slowly turned her hand in his. She hadn't heard him come back.

"It looks like you're going to have a blood blister," he

said at last, gently rubbing the tip of her finger. He didn't release her hand, and his failure to do so filled her with a warm sweetness. "I'm beginning to think this isn't your sport. First you hurt your ankle and now your finger."

Deftly he knelt down, unbuckled her boots himself, and slipped them from her feet. "Which ankle did you hurt?"

"The left one."

He examined it carefully. His expertise reminded her of Tim, who'd been a surgeon, and prompted her to question, "Are you a doctor?"

"I nearly was, but I got married my last year in medical school and dropped out." He switched back to the present. "Your ankle doesn't seem to be broken. I think it'll be fine in a couple of days."

Married! Not for a minute had it occurred to her he might be married. An odd pain sliced through her.

"Your wife . . ." Leslie stumbled. "Is she . . ."

"She's dead," came the curt reply. Suddenly the warmth died in his black gaze, and all the shuttered bitterness was back in the harsh planes of his face.

"I'm sorry. . . ." She broke off. The words sounded so hollow somehow. "I didn't realize . . ."

"It happened over a year ago," he explained tersely. "Her car stalled on a railroad crossing, and a train hit it. She died instantly."

That hot angry look was back in his face, and he regarded her intently as though she were somehow the cause of his pain. Leslie realized that he was used to guarding his privacy and hadn't wanted to share this with her. Yet he had.

"You ready?" he asked impatiently, and when she nodded, his arm slipped possessively around her and he drew her to her feet. Just his casual touch stimulated fiery sensations that made her feel strangely weak.

He picked up her ski boots as well as his own, and together they stepped outside into the whirling white snow.

As he lifted their skis from the rack onto his shoulders he spoke again.

"Don't ask me about my wife," he said. "She belongs to a chapter in my life that's closed forever."

Quietly she responded, "I think I understand."

"No, you don't!" He ground out the words with startling violence. "You couldn't possibly, and if we're to get on at all, don't even try."

2

~~~~~~~~~~~~~~~~~~~~~~

Through thick bristly lashes, Leslie glanced covertly at Boone, who was skillfully driving his truck over the snow-packed highway toward Winter Park. A winter wonderland whisked by, but she was aware only of the compelling, virile man beside her. One of his powerful arms was draped across the back of their seat so that every time she moved her tousled curls brushed against it.

Ever since the mention of his wife, Boone had been broodingly silent, and she hadn't been able to think of a word to say. Several more miles sped by before Boone made an attempt to bridge the awkward silence. Then she felt his fingers caress her hair, and she sensed he was suddenly more conscious of the woman beside him than the woman he'd once been married to.

"So, tell me about yourself," he said at last as though conversation were a deliberate effort. "Are you in Winter Park as a tourist?"

"I live here."

"Then how have I missed seeing you? With only four hundred locals it's sort of hard not to bump into one another rather frequently."

"I just moved here from Texas."

"And I've been away in Denver this past month. That explains it. Tell me, are you married?"

"Divorced."

"Isn't everybody?" A trace of the old bitterness was back in his cold tone. His cynical statement caught her off guard, and she didn't know how to reply. "I suppose marriage is too confining for people these days," he continued. "With women's lib and the sexual revolution, who wants to stay married to the same person for an entire lifetime?"

She had. . . . His words, so close to Tim's beliefs, chilled her. "I suppose there's an element of truth in what you say," she admitted, feeling numb.

"More than an element," he snapped. "Why did you leave your own husband?"

Involuntarily she flinched. "Why did *you* leave . . ." He took it for granted that it was she who had walked out. The old hurt tore through her, but she covered it with anger.

"*That* is none of your business!" Her eyes felt hot, and she fought back the tears.

Through the shimmering haze of unfallen tears, she saw his swift dark glance in her direction.

Switching the topic to neutral ground, Boone's deep

voice was devoid of emotion when he spoke again. "We're almost to town. You'll have to tell me where you live. . . ."

Carefully, in a tiny, choked voice she directed him to a modern stack of cedar condominiums clumped on the snowy side of a mountain beneath a cluster of towering lodgepole pines. When he braked to a stop in front of her garage, Leslie reached for the door handle and would have stumbled from the pickup, but Boone's hand closed warmly over hers.

"Don't go," he said thickly. "Not yet. . . . I've been damn near impossible ever since we met. And I shouldn't have asked such a personal question a while ago. I should know that better than anyone."

His dark face was grave. The genuine sincerity of his apology touched her heart. "It's all right," she whispered at last, letting her emerald gaze fuse with the liquid blackness of his own.

"It seems that the past is dangerous ground for us both," he murmured against her ear. His warm breath sent delicious shivers down her spine. This new intimacy was strangely comforting.

"Yes . . ." she whispered against the stiff collar of his parka.

"I find the present much much more interesting," he said huskily, pulling her into his arms.

For an instant he stared deeply into her eyes as though to drink in the sight of her. Then very slowly his dark head descended to her fair one. His hot moist mouth covered the lush softness of her lips, and a raw, naked hunger for his touch leaped through her. Tiny waves of liquid passion curled in her veins. She wrapped her arms around his neck and ran her fingers through his thick springy hair.

He felt her fiery response, the warmth of her desperate need for him.

"Oh, Leslie . . ." he rasped. "I knew the minute I saw you I was lost. . . ."

Strange words. . . . Yet she'd felt the same way.

But she forgot everything as he crushed her slim body against his own virile length. His breathing was harsh and uneven, his male scent touched her nostrils. She felt the powerful surge of his desire against her lower body, but the flaming onslaught of his savage passion only heightened her own burning ache. She returned his kisses with a wanton abandon, crushing her lips fervently to his. Her fingers reveled in the exploration of his magnificent physique, in the hard pressure of his lean, muscled frame tightly pressed to the tender softness of her own body.

"It's been too long . . . for both of us," he rasped. "We're like two starved . . ." He didn't finish as his mouth again nuzzled hers. She felt his tongue probe and enter and touch her own deliberately. His hands swept over the soft mounds of her breasts and downward to her rounded hips and molded her body even closer to his own.

From behind them a horn tooted impatiently. Slowly Boone dragged his lips from hers and studied her love-soft face with vision blurred from desire. "I'm going to have to move the truck," he said raggedly as the tiny foreign car bleated again.

As if in a dream, Leslie was aware of his deft movements as he slid his body away from hers and started the ignition of the truck. His thick black hair was rumpled from their loveplay; a trace of her lipstick lingered on his lips.

What was happening to her? Was this love at first sight? Or was it lust? Doubtless her response to this man had been heightened by the long months of despair and loneliness. But to find such rapture in the arms of a stranger was inexplicable.

Boone found a parking place directly in front of her condominium this time. When he cut off the ignition, he did not take her in his arms again. Instead he alighted from the truck and went around and opened her door. His arms slid around her waist, and he helped her down. Then he reached behind her and gathered up her ski boots. "I'll come back for your skis later," he explained as he followed her inside the building to her front door.

He took the key from her fingers and opened the door for her. For a long moment they stood in awkward silence as a furious mental debate raged in her mind. After those sizzling kisses, if she asked him in, he would take it as an open invitation to make love to her. And she wasn't sure she was ready for that, even though every fiber in her body clamored for his touch.

As though he read her mind, he said, "Leslie, I'm not going to ravish you if you ask me in."

"I didn't think you would," she said, flushing. "Of course, I want you to come in."

"Thank you." His amused smile had a devastating impact on her senses.

"Can I fix you something to drink?"

"I'd like a beer. But I can get it myself."

When she opened the refrigerator he was directly behind her. The two steaks she'd been too tired to broil last night for herself and Karen were in full view. She needed to cook them soon or they would spoil.

"Would you like to stay for dinner?" she asked, knowing but not caring that he thought she probably was inviting him to more than dinner.

His virile masculinity was like a fine wine that had gone to her head. She was enjoying his company too much to want him to leave, even though she sensed his continued presence meant danger.

"I thought you'd never ask," he murmured. His hand reached up and straightened a stray golden curl, but when she turned and gazed into his eyes, he let his hand fall quickly away. "If I touch you again, I won't be able to stop," he said in explanation. "And I'm sure after skiing all day you're as hungry as I am."

His eyes held hers, and when she said nothing she realized that her silence held a promise. The sensual tension between them was explosive, and a rippling excitement coursed through Leslie before she forced herself to look away.

"I'll start dinner," she said shakily.

"And I'll build a fire," he returned.

Then he lifted the beer can to his lips and deliberately moved away from her, breaking the spell that had bound them together.

The stainless blade flashed as Leslie rapidly sliced the head of lettuce into pale green strips that fluttered into the salad bowl on the kitchen counter. Covertly she observed Boone as he tossed another log onto the fire.

The mere sight of him—so overwhelmingly male— triggered a nervous yet pleasurable excitement in her. He looked up from the fire, and his eyes met hers.

At Boone's insistence she'd changed from her ski attire into "something more comfortable." She now wore a loosely flowing, emerald green caftan. The thick velour was trimmed with gilt. A rope sash cinched her tiny waist.

"Need any help with dinner?" he asked.

"No, just relax. It's almost ready."

Minutes later he helped her into her chair and then seated himself. "You've prepared a feast!" he said in admiration as he looked at the broiled steaks, the crisp, tossed salad, baked potatoes, creamy green beans garnished with mushrooms, and hot buttered rolls.

"Not without the help of my microwave," she admitted shyly.

His compliment warmed her. It had been a long time since she'd cooked for a man. All Karen ever really liked was peanut butter and jelly. Leslie flashed him a warm, appreciative smile and murmured a trembling, "Thank you."

"I can see you're a very talented woman. You've done wonders with this place." His admiring gaze swept from her lovely face about the ultra-modern condominium, where cascading green plants and bold paintings accented the decor.

"Thank you. . . ."

"It seems you're always saying thank you," he said, slicing into his thick steak.

"And do you live in Winter Park, Boone?" she asked, changing the subject from herself to him.

"Most of the time—for the past five years. Winter Park is a boom town, and I'm working on several projects here at the moment."

Before she could reply, something on the television

arrested his attention, and he got up and turned up the volume.

". . . and that's it folks," the newscaster blared. "We're in for a heavy snowfall throughout the evening and into tomorrow. So bundle up and stay inside. . . ."

Boone switched off the set and strode restlessly to the expanse of glass beside the fireplace. Pulling back the drapes, he peered outside. Steady flurries of snow sifted in the pale stream of the electric light on her balcony. "Doesn't look too bad," he said. "At least not yet. Those newscasters are fond of melodrama."

At that moment a faint blast echoed through the mountains followed by a series of three more.

"What was that?" Leslie asked.

"The avalanche-control people are setting off dynamite charges in the mountains to cause small avalanches."

"Small avalanches?" A faint note of alarm crept into her voice.

He turned to her, his expression gentle. "It's nothing to worry about. In fact, it's because of those blasts that we don't have to worry. During a storm, when fresh snow falls onto old, it has to be constantly monitored and small avalanches triggered to prevent larger ones. Unfortunately, because of all the new development and expansion, we're becoming more vulnerable to the threat of avalanches."

Boone sat down once more and resumed eating.

"Do you live far from here?" Leslie asked, changing the subject.

"About half a mile," he returned. "But in a blizzard, it might as well be all the way to Denver."

They talked throughout the meal, and she was aware that, though he learned much about her, she learned practically nothing of him. She told him of Karen, her child, and how difficult quitting her teaching job and moving from Austin was for her.

"Sounds like you're determined to burn your bridges," he said at length, his eyes filled with understanding. "If I weren't so damned tied to Winter Park I would have left myself. But every cent I've got is tied up here, and I have no choice but to stay."

"You're probably as well off," she said softly. "I'm beginning to realize there are some things you can't run away from."

"How right you are." His sensual lips twisted into a hard line as he poured himself another glass of wine. "But sometimes, you can forget for a while." He caught her frightened glance and held it. The hungry brilliance of his black gaze startled her, and a delicate flush suffused her creamy skin before she quickly lowered her long-lashed eyes. He lifted the glass to his lips and then rose slowly from the table.

She felt his fingers roam beneath her heavy hair and caress her neck before they descended to the back of her chair. A prickle of desire flamed through her. "Let's enjoy the fire, shall we?" His deep voice had roughened slightly with emotion.

No more able to resist his invitation than a moth the brilliance of a flame, she allowed his arms to slide around her as she stood up. She was aware of her heart beating crazily. His dark intimate gaze made her feel oddly warm, as together they moved toward the fire.

Firelight made her hair gleam like tawny gold; her

emerald eyes sparkled as she gazed up into his own dark eyes.

She was bewitchingly beautiful, and she only had the faintest idea of her power over him. As he moved his calloused hand from her throat down over her arm and back again in a slow stroking motion, he found her soft body as smooth as satin. He crushed his lips into her thick, flowing hair.

Ah, the scent of her. . . . She was delicious.

As he pulled her down beneath him on the deep plush carpet, he momentarily forgot the anguish that had tormented him every waking minute for a year. Her soft body offered oblivion, offered a surcease however brief from his pain.

For her his embrace assuaged the deep loneliness that had engulfed her since Tim had walked out. When Boone's mouth touched hers in a lengthy, searing kiss, she felt fused to him. The long, lonely months were swept away as his arms locked around her body, and she felt a hot passionate need licking through her.

The rounded sweetness of her body was pressed hard against the lean, tough sweep of his own. Her lips quivered beneath his as he kissed her again and again.

In a daze of sexual desire she felt the warmth of his hands caress her throat, and then very carefully they slid the zipper of her gown downward, parting the velvety emerald softness so that the opulent fruit of her body was revealed to his heated gaze.

"Oh, God . . . Leslie . . . you're so beautiful. . . ."

Slowly he removed the gown, sliding it over the luscious curve of her hips until it lay, a velvety puddle, about her slender ankles. Her own fingers pushed his ski sweater upward, and deftly he shrugged out of it. Quickly he removed his trousers and he lay beside her. She caught her breath at the sight of so much exposed virile masculinity. Not an ounce of spare flesh marred his lean physique. He lay before her like some dark-skinned, princely savage—pagan and proud, latently ruthless.

Tenderly his fingers stroked her breasts, and then his lips followed where his hands had roamed. She felt his hard, sensual mouth, nibbling the tips of her breasts; she felt the moist sucking of his lips against her tender flesh. A tiny moan escaped her lips, as a spasm of exquisite pleasure shivered through her. She arched her body so that it fitted more tightly against his own. Her hands trailed through the thick darkness of his hair.

His fingertips moved lightly over her with the expertise of a skilled lover who knew where and how to touch a woman so that she reveled in dizzying sensual ecstacy. Again his mouth followed the path of his hands, reverently loving her, touching her in all the most intimate places, rousing her long-dormant sensuality until she was as wild with passion as he.

Then he was crushing her beneath him as though he couldn't contain his desire any longer.

"Marnie . . ." Boone whispered desperately into her hair. "Oh, Marnie . . . Marnie . . ."

Leslie froze in his arms. For a long moment his deep tortured utterance was the only sound in the room save for their mutual labored breathing. Then a log tumbled in the grate, and a shower of sparks popped.

Shivering and numbed, Leslie tried to draw away, but Boone caught her wrist and drew her slim body against his.

"That was a pretty bad slip, Leslie," he murmured

against her earlobe. She lay like a stiff, wooden doll against him. "But that shouldn't spoil . . ."

"It did." The words were a tiny, strangled sound. She tried to choke back the hot pain that welled in her.

"I don't blame you if you're angry . . ." he continued huskily.

"I'm not angry, Boone," she said very quietly. "It's just that I see clearly that this . . ." Her fingers combed the matted hair of his chest. "That we were wrong . . ."

"Wrong?"

"Wrong to get so involved so quickly. We're making love for all the wrong reasons. I've been so lonely that I just . . . I couldn't say no to you even though I should have. And you wanted to pretend I was your wife. . . ."

"Pretend *you* were my wife!" he rasped. Genuine shock laced his deep, cold tones as he pushed her from him in disgust and sat up. "If that's what you thought, you're very wrong!"

"Then what?"

"I thought I could forget," he muttered furiously. His saturnine glance swept the golden curves of her body gleaming in the soft light. "And maybe I still can . . ."

"Please, Boone . . ."

"I have to have you." In the flickering firelight Boone's chiseled features were harsh and ruthlessly compelling. He looked like a bronzed pagan god. The message in his boldly hot black gaze was primitive and wild.

Fear pounded through Leslie's arteries as he dragged her into the electric warmth of his arms.

"Boone, don't . . . not now. . . . I'm afraid."

"You don't need to be. All I'm going to do is make love to you."

3

꩜

All I'm going to do is make love to you. . . . Boone's words thundered through Leslie as she tried to shrink away. But he moved faster than she and placed an elbow on either side of her shoulders, leaning over her so that she was imprisoned in his arms. Her golden hair spilled in tangled disarray over his hands; wispy tendrils of it were matted against her face. Green eyes glimmered like liquid jewels as she stared up into his darkly handsome visage.

Her heart beat with the delicate ferocity of a frightened rabbit's. Her breaths came in harsh, rapid gasps so that the tips of her breasts rose and fell against the bristly hairs that matted the hard warmth of his chest.

His muscles about her were like iron. She twisted in a vain attempt to free herself, but her every movement only brought her into more intimate contact with his virile body. Every time she touched him it was like an electric shock wave rippling through her. She felt him shudder and clasp her more tightly to him.

Slowly Boone lowered himself over her, so that it seemed that every part of her felt the fierce raging heat of his body against her own. In spite of her desperation in the deepest part of her soul she registered the fleeting sensation that this savage mating with this tall dark stranger was meant to be.

His black head descended with deliberate slowness to hers. Cruelly ravaging the lush softness of her lips, Boone forced them open so that his tongue could plunder the velvety depths of her mouth. She doubled her fists to beat at him, but his long drugging kiss devoured her resistance. Her hands that would have struck him fell away and lay limply on the thick carpet. As the strength to fight him slowly ebbed from her, the forcefulness of his assault gave way to fierce tenderness.

In spite of herself, Leslie felt her body responding to the gentle rain of kisses on her mouth, against her throat, in her tumbling hair. His caressing hands moving over her filled her body with a strange, flowing warmth until she clung to him with breathless urgency. When he at last drew away a tiny moan of disappointment escaped her love-bruised lips.

"Tell me you want me," he commanded. His voice against the softness of her skin was low and deep.

At first she did not comprehend, her senses spiraling in a state of sensuous nirvana. He lowered his lips and kissed her half-opened mouth again, his tongue plunging into its satiny-warm interior. Leslie twined her arms around his neck to hold him even closer, and his hot, demanding lips brought forth a little cry of sheer, feminine rapture.

Lifting his head once more, he repeated his command. "Say it! Tell me!"

Very gently Leslie breathed, "I want you. Oh, I do want you so. . . . Please . . . make love to me."

The grooves beside his mouth deepened as a faint smile curved his lips. When Boone took her in his arms again the lovers were both consumed by the savage fires of their desire. His heart pulsed in tempo with the wild drumbeat of her own as he drew her higher and higher in a soaring swirl of need.

For a timeless moment it seemed that they had always known one another, that each belonged only to the other. When he possessed her fully, she cried out his name in final surrender.

A draft of cool air stirred the tumbling masses of Leslie's hair, and drowsily she curled herself into a languid ball beneath the thermal blanket that had been carefully tucked about her. The click of the front door closing brought her instantly awake.

For an instant, in a dazed state of confusion, she stared about the room. Then her eyes fell on the rich jewel-green caftan swirled at her feet. She saw Boone's half-empty wineglass on the hearth, and a hot rush of color washed over her as everything came back to her.

Dreamily she recalled the passionate lovemaking that was the cause of her euphoric state. Where was Boone? Her hands groped for his warmth, and finding nothing but the cool thickness of the plush carpet, a terrible emptiness engulfed her.

He was gone. A spasm of pain like a sliver of glass cutting tender flesh sliced her heart.

Where was he? Again her eyes scanned the silent room, but he was not there. Then she remembered the clicking sound the door had made. He must have gone out. The fire had burned low, and there was only one more log on the hearth.

Languidly she lay back and thought over what had happened. She had given herself freely to a man she hardly knew. And yet already she knew that this man was special to her. From the moment she'd set eyes on him, he'd compelled her deepest feelings. It was all very difficult for her to understand because nothing like this had ever happened to her.

With Tim her feelings had developed gradually; there had not been this immediate yearning. Boone's touch, his lovemaking, his ability to draw her out of herself with such devastating completeness was out of the realm of her experience. Even after eight years of marriage, she'd never felt that she so totally belonged to a man.

She'd given a part of herself that irrevocably belonged to him. It had been like fainting, like death itself, and she knew that she would never be the same again.

Had she been stupid to give herself so completely— and on the first night that she'd met him? She'd never done anything like this before. Never had it even occurred to her that she was capable of such powerful feelings for a man she'd just met. Her good judgment told her it would have been much more sensible to get to know him as a person before letting him make love to her. And yet she couldn't have stopped herself, and for some reason, she didn't regret it. No matter what happened, their coming together had been too beautiful for regret. Idly she wondered what Boone was thinking and feeling right now.

At the sound of a man's heavy tread on the stair outside, she started. The front door was shoved open and quickly shut, as a gust of cold air seeped inside. Wildly Leslie whirled, and her gaze locked with Boone's fierce black one. A faint depression settled over her as she saw that the haunted bitterness was back in the grim lines of his handsome face.

Snowflakes glistened in the thick tousled darkness of his hair. In his arms he held three snow-crusted logs.

"It's only me," came his deep, curt drawl. "I'm sorry I woke you up."

He was kneeling beside her and putting another log in the grate. "Looks like I'll be spending the night," he said offhandedly. "I shouldn't have left the truck out in this snowstorm. My snow tires are too worn for me to try to make it down the hill until the street's plowed in the morning."

He offered no words of endearment. He merely attended to the practical task of unloading the firewood.

An involuntary blush swept her when his knowing gaze roamed over her, lingering on the creamy flesh of her breast exposed where the blanket had fallen away. Suddenly her heart was beating too fast, and again she wondered what he was thinking. This night had been such a novel experience that she felt vaguely embarrassed.

In no time the fire was an enormous blaze, flooding the room with its warmth. When Boone finished, he knelt beside her and wrapped one of his arms around her. Gently he brushed the thick strands of her hair to one

38

side so that it cascaded over her bare shoulders. "Did anyone ever tell you how beautiful you are . . . when you wake up after making love?" he murmured huskily.

Did he assume nights like this were commonplace to her? A strange uneasiness filled her.

"No," she replied softly. "You may not believe this, but you're the first man since my husband to . . ."

"I believe you. But just because it happened, I wouldn't read more into it than there is." There was a tense bitterness in his tone that made her feel unhappy.

"B-but . . ." The one word quivered in the air. "Are you saying that . . . that you spend nights like this with lots of women, that I meant nothing to you?"

Just the thought made her feel wretched. He saw the pain in her eyes.

"No." His negative reply was terse; his forbidding expression told her nothing.

"Then what do you mean?" For some reason it was very important to her to understand this man.

"I don't know why it's so difficult to figure out. What happened tonight . . . just happened. I don't know why. Nothing exactly like this has ever happened to me before. Look, I don't want to hurt your feelings by what I'm going to say . . ." He broke off, feeling uncomfortable. Her large green eyes never left his face. "I only know that I don't want to be involved with you or any other woman—not deeply anyway. Tonight didn't change that. It's not that I have anything against you personally."

"I see," she murmured quietly, very hurt by his attitude.

"Look, if you'll only try to see things from my point of view we'll get on fine," he continued. "There's no reason why we can't continue to enjoy dating one another. I just want you to understand I'm not interested in a serious relationship with anyone—not even you."

She was beginning to understand too well, and she didn't like what he was saying one bit.

"We'll get on fine. . . ." she hurled back in a tight whisper. "How can you say that when you just said that what happened between us meant nothing?"

"You were good. I don't deny that," he stated coolly. His heated gaze raking her made her go hot with shame. "We were good together. I needed what you had to offer, but that's all I want from you . . . or any other woman— ever. You're hardly an eighteen-year-old virgin. You're an adult with a life of your own, a child to raise, a bad marriage in your past. I doubt you're any more interested in entanglements than I am, and if you're honest, you won't try to pretend that you feel any differently than I do."

"But I do. . . . I do. . . ." she thought weakly, but pride kept this admission a silent one.

"What turned you against women?" she asked softly.

His deep voice responded, and with every word she felt he killed a tiny fragment of her soul.

"A lifetime of observation and first-hand experience. I won't bore you by elaborating further."

"I want to know," she demanded. "If my entire sex is damned in your eyes I want to know why."

"All right. You asked for it." She was startled by the raw anger in his voice. His eyes blazed as he looked down at her, but suddenly she had the oddest feeling it was no longer her he was seeing or thinking of, but someone else. "The women I've known have only wanted to wreck any man they got close to. And are you really any different?" His hand reached out and gently caressed the line of her throat. "You're very lovely, but on the inside what are you like?" Slowly he withdrew his hand and gave her a long searching look.

His eyes never left her face. His low voice continued, "The minute I saw you I wanted you, and you knew it. I saw the hunger in your eyes. You looked lonely and vulnerable—beautiful and aloof. And yet with me tonight you were hot and passionate. You even seem sweet. But women are rarely what they seem, especially beautiful ones."

She felt the pain in his voice, and she wanted to reach out to him, to make him understand somehow that even though he'd been hurt in the past, he shouldn't consider all women in such a biased light. Men could tear up lives as well as women. How well she knew.

His lips twisted cynically, and his voice was harsh. "Tell me, are you like the women I've known? Did you leave your husband broken-hearted when you got tired of marriage and wanted more excitement?"

"No!" she breathed. "It wasn't like that."

"Or were you—what is it all you women are doing these days—finding yourself? Is that why you left him?"

"No. . . ." The word was a whisper which he didn't hear.

Suddenly it was no longer Leslie the person he was speaking to but Leslie as the physical embodiment of women in general. He wanted to hurt as he'd been hurt. "And what did you find in bed with me tonight?" he lashed.

"Oooo . . ." The wretched cry of anguish wrenched from the depths of her wounded heart was punctuated

41

with the cracking sound her palm made against his tanned cheek. Her hand throbbed with pain. Where she'd struck him, there was a deep red mark.

He caught her wrist, and his eyes gleamed with anger. "Don't ever hit me again," he warned. Her violent action had at least served to bring him back to the present and made him aware of her as an individual once more.

She pulled her hand free from his grasp, shocked at what she'd done. Never had she hit anyone before.

"I-I'm sorry," she murmured. "But I'm not like what you said! I'm not! You don't know me!"

"Look, maybe I put things a little too brutally," he went on more gently, genuinely apologetic. "Sometimes I get a little carried away on that subject." He attempted a smile. "But I met someone once, someone you reminded me of before, and she got inside me and destroyed . . ." His deep voice had become almost vengeful. "I'll never let another woman close again."

He was speaking of his wife, of course, Leslie thought. He'd loved her and her death had devastated him. No wonder. . . . Leslie's heart softened toward him in spite of everything he'd said.

His dark eyes held hers. "I wanted you even though I didn't want to," he admitted. "But that's all there'll ever be between us."

"No commitment," she sighed wearily. That's exactly what Tim had said he'd wanted. Was every man singing that same song?

"That's right," came his terse reply.

"That's just fine with me," she said shakily.

The last thing she wanted was to get involved with another man like Tim, no matter how compellingly attractive he was to her. In a way she should be grateful to Boone for telling her the way he felt right from the beginning. It had been a mistake to sleep with him before she understood him, of course. But it was a mistake she didn't have to compound by getting any more deeply involved. She'd learned a very bitter lesson.

He traced a fingertip along her shoulder blade, and she shivered as a molten tingle quivered through her. "I'm glad we understand each other," he said, not understanding her at all as he reached to pull her into his arms.

"Don't touch me," she cried, shrugging out of his embrace and ignoring the treacherous leap of her pulse at his touch.

"It's going to be a long, cold night, and I have no intention of sleeping alone," he said huskily, his dark mood vanishing as he thought of holding her in his arms once more.

She was very aware of his lean muscled frame stretching indolently beside hers.

"Well, I do."

"It's a little late in the day for virginal protestations," he said gruffly, letting his hand trail downward over the satiny skin on her arm.

"Nevertheless, you're sleeping on the couch," she insisted, trying to ignore the tiny ache the thought of not sleeping wrapped in the warmth of his arms produced.

"I guess you know this is the oldest trick in the book," he said, keeping his tone even.

"What?"

"Coming on hot and heavy and then acting like a coy miss. You think that after sampling the goods I'll do anything to have you again."

His insolence was suddenly unbearable.

"Oh, shut up," she snapped furiously. "I'm tired of you telling me what I'm like and what I think. If you'd listen to me for one minute I'd tell you myself what I'm like."

He infuriated her all the more by listening to her with a wicked gleam in his eye. A broad smile spread lazily across his tanned features as he noticed the way she trembled and the way her lips pursed in a provocative pout.

"You're even beautiful when you're mad," he whispered, deliberately baiting her.

"In the morning," she choked. She could scarcely look at him any longer she was so angry. "I want you to get out of my house and out of my life for good. I'm not interested in any sort of relationship with you because I've known men like you before myself. And I'm sick of them."

With that she gathered her caftan about her and stormed from the room.

Behind her she heard his mocking laughter. "Suit yourself, little spitfire. But if you change your mind, you know where to find me."

Even though it was still dark outside when Leslie woke, Boone was already gone. Wearily she straightened the condominium until there was no sign that he had ever been there. If only she could wipe him from her mind and heart as easily.

For a long moment her eyes lingered on the blanket strewn in front of the fireplace before she picked it up and folded it, replacing it in the closet. She'd certainly made a mess of things. Why, she'd made love to a man, and she didn't even know his name. If only . . . She caught herself. She had no time for *if only's*. With fierce determination she pushed last night and Boone from her mind.

A quick look at her calendar reminded her that Mr. Carson would be coming over at ten o'clock. He was a wealthy Texas oilman in Winter Park for a week-long ski vacation with his family. She'd shown him several pieces of property, and he'd called early yesterday morning to say he wanted to talk to her.

Dressing with special care to look attractive, she eyed herself critically in the full-length mirror of her bedroom. An extra layer of light makeup had been needed to erase the dark shadows that had lingered beneath her eyes because of her sleepless night. But other than that she was pleased with her appearance. It gave her a measure of pleasure to imagine Tim's response. He would have been shocked. Gone was the brown wren look she'd once affected. Instead she was a brightly garbed parrot; she was the glamour girl he'd taunted she could never be.

Her golden hair was caught in a flame-colored scarf that matched her flame silk blouse. A long, delicate, golden chain swung between the hollow of her full breasts, which were tantalyzingly revealed because several buttons of her blouse were undone. She wore a dark brown, tightly fitting wool skirt that had a long slit up the back. Every time she moved, shapely legs encased in nylon stockings were displayed. Over one arm she slung a matching jacket.

She experienced the oddest momentary sensation that the girl in the mirror wasn't really she herself at all. For all her exterior polish, inside she was still the same plain girl she'd always been. Then the doorbell buzzed, putting an end to her reflections.

Mr. Carson shifted his bifocals as he studied the blueprints of several condominiums laid out on Leslie's diningroom table. An untouched cup of coffee steamed beside him. Smoke curled from a crystal ashtray. "I can't make up my mind which plan to go with," he fumed.

"If you pick the D plan, you'll have four bedrooms and a view of the Continental Divide," Leslie inserted pleasantly.

He sighed. "That view certainly is spectacular. But my wife hates to walk upstairs."

"Then perhaps the B plan would be better. You'd be right over the garage and near the Jacuzzi . . ."

"This fellow you work for, R.B. Dexter, certainly is a quality builder. I think I'll buy the whole building," he decided. "That'll save me from having to make a decision."

"All four condominiums," she breathed. Excitement coursed through her. This would be her first real sale.

"One for myself and the other three as investments," Mr. Carson continued calmly. "It's hard to pass up below-market interest rates. What time tomorrow can I make an appointment at your office to sign an earnest money contract?"

"Why, any time, Mr. Carson," she beamed. "Any time at all . . ."

At just that minute the doorbell buzzed. "Now who could that be?" she murmured distractedly. She didn't expect Karen until after lunch. "Excuse me, Mr. Carson." She flashed him the warmest of smiles.

"Sure, honey. . . ." Absently he nodded his silver head.

As soon as she unbolted the lock, the door was pushed open by the tall dark man on the other side of it. The mere sight of him tore through her nervous system like a jagged pain.

"Boone!" She paled even as she was aware of a tiny pulsebeat pounding in her throat.

His face was haggard and drawn. Fleetingly she wondered if he'd gotten as little sleep as she. He hadn't shaved yet, and the lines beneath his eyes were more deeply cut than they had been last night. But to her he was the most handsome sight in the world. He wore jeans and a sheepskin coat. The top two buttons of his flannel plaid shirt were unbuttoned, revealing the dark hairs that grew thickly on his tanned chest. In his arms he carried a dozen long-stemmed red roses.

"I-I didn't think you'd . . ." Overwhelmed, she choked on her words. Had he come back because he cared more than he was capable of admitting?

His wandering gaze was dark with an indefinable emotion. His eyes slowly roamed over her, over the delicate features of her face, her exquisite long-lashed eyes, her lush, pearly lips, then down the column of her throat, lingering where her golden filigree chain plunged to the soft hollow between her breasts. The intensity of his gaze made her skin tingle with an odd warmth as if his mere look were a physical caress.

She hadn't known until this moment how much this man, a stranger, meant to her. She was weak with joy.

"Who'd you expect?" he demanded gruffly.

"I—I . . ."

"Certainly not me. That's for sure," he said dryly. "I

would have called first, but I didn't know your last name. Can I come in?"

Behind her Mr. Carson rustled several papers with an air of impatience. "I, well . . ." she stammered. "I'm afraid I'm busy right now." She flushed deeply, feeling acutely uncomfortable for fear he would misinterpret the situation. "Perhaps . . . later . . ."

Boone's swift dark gaze took in at a glance Mr. Carson's coat strewn casually across a stuffed armchair. Though he couldn't see the other man from where he stood, Boone caught the scent of tobacco that had not been in the condominium last night permeating the air.

"I see," he said curtly, not seeing at all. His dark face was harshly forbidding. "Like I said, I should have called first." He tossed the flowers into her shaking arms. "Keep these."

A thorn pricked her fingers, but she didn't notice. Wincing at the savage violence in his tone, at the fierce anger blazing in his eyes, she pleaded softly, "Boone. . . . It's not what you think. I . . ."

"You can save your explanations for the next poor fool that falls for you," he returned roughly.

"Boone . . ." But he ignored the soft sound of her voice falling after him as he stalked rapidly down the hall out into the white, winter day and was gone.

Slowly she closed the door.

"Boyfriend trouble?" Mr. Carson nodded sagely.

"You might call it that," she said wearily, depositing the scarlet bundle of flowers into the sink. Then she returned to the table and feigned a bright smile.

"Child, you've cut yourself," Mr. Carson said kindly, groping for his handkerchief, which he promptly located. "Here . . ."

She pressed the handkerchief to her bleeding hand. Mr. Carson's plump, kindly face swam before her. "Mr. Carson, I'm sorry," she said brokenly. "I . . . I can't go on."

"I understand. I think we've made all the important decisions today. I'll be at your office," he paused to check a tiny black notebook he was carrying, "at ten again tomorrow. Will that be all right with you?"

"Perfectly," she said gratefully as he rose and showed himself to the door.

When he had gone she sank into the plump cushions of her couch. Boone had come back, but nothing had changed between them. He'd leapt immediately to the wrong conclusion without giving her a chance to explain. It seemed he was determined to think poorly of her.

If she were smart she would forget him; she was certain that she had seen the last of him.

4

Carefully Leslie studied the earnest money contract that she'd had the contract department draw up. Everything seemed to be in order, but she decided she'd better get Tad Wood to take a look, just in case she'd missed something. She rose from her desk and moved swiftly from her office into the hall and then knocked on Tad's office.

"Come in. . . ."

She pushed the door open.

"Hello, beautiful," Tad gushed, laughingly. His blue eyes roamed her feminine curves clad in clinging blue silk. "If I'd known it was you I would have done a handspring over the desk to get that door open. . . ."

Suddenly Leslie's warm laughter joined his. "I was wondering if you'd take a look at . . ."

"What the . . ." The unfinished question hung in the

air like thunder before a storm. From behind her the deep, all-too-familiar voice sent shock waves rippling through Leslie's nervous system. She whirled to meet Boone's savage, penetrating black stare that stripped her to the very depths of her soul. She gasped. The contract fluttered through her fingers to the floor, but she was unaware that it had done so.

As if in a dream she heard Tad's friendly, "R.B., when did you get back in town?"

"Friday night," came the deep, cold voice that chilled every nerve fiber in her being. His black gaze never left her face.

"R.B." Leslie's mind floundered. Were Boone and R.B. Dexter, her boss, one and the same person?

"I guess you haven't met Leslie Grant yet," Tad said, unaware of the seething undercurrents. "Les, this is R.B. Dexter. R.B., we were so short-handed since Roger quit and you were away that your mother hired Les to fill in while you were gone."

"Mother did what?"

"She hired Les."

"On whose authority? Everyone knows I do the hiring around here."

"But you weren't here, R.B.," Rose Mary Dexter interjected placidly in a softly cajoling voice from behind them. Silently she'd stepped from her own office to join the group in the hall. "Son, it's good to have you back," Rose Mary said, her vivacious black eyes sparkling. In her red and white dress she looked just like Mrs. Santa Claus and just as guileless. "Why didn't you call and let me know you were home?" Her cheeks dimpled as her face was illuminated by a cheery smile.

"I . . . er . . ." Boone's hot gaze lingered on Leslie.

51

"Something came up, Mother, . . . unexpectedly," he finished offhandedly. An involuntary blush stained Leslie's cheeks a deep red, and she forced herself to concentrate on the chipped tip of a fingernail. "I want to speak to Mrs. Grant alone," he continued smoothly, masking his anger. "If you two don't mind?"

"Not at all," his mother demurred.

A trembling weakness spread through Leslie's body as she scurried quickly behind Boone, who was heading rapidly down the hall toward his office. Once they were both inside, he shut the door behind them.

Leslie was only dimly aware of rich dark paneling, thick carpet, and a gleaming oak desk. Her eyes devoured the sight of Boone as he towered before her—so ruthlessly male, so formidably angry.

"I should have known the minute I saw you, this was a setup." His face was dark with hostility.

"A what?" Astonishment widened her eyes.

"Don't pull that 'Little Miss Innocent' act on me again!" he growled. "It nearly worked Saturday night, but it won't work again!"

"Boone, I don't have the slightest idea what you're talking about."

"Don't you? Then let me spell it out for you. You knew who I was all along. You knew that when I took one look at you I could scarcely ignore you. This is a deliberate plot. . . ."

"I don't know what you're talking about," she repeated.

"Don't worry. I intend to have a long talk with my mother and get to the bottom of this."

"Boone, I . . ."

"You're fired. There's no way I want you working for me. Do you understand?"

"But I signed a contract."

"It isn't worth the paper it's written on without my signature." Though his voice was soft, it was laced with icy coldness.

"Boone, what is going on?" a deep frown creased her brow. "I'd never seen you before until Saturday at the ski slope. What makes you think . . ."

"For your information, this isn't the first time Mother's tried to find a woman for me. It seems she's determined to see me married again. You're not the first woman she's hired with this purpose in mind. I suppose she wants grandchildren. But this time she went too far." His voice was hard and filled with anger.

"Boone . . ." She was desperate to understand what he was talking about.

Suddenly he ripped his gaze from her lovely features and strode to the far side of his desk. Then he rummaged furiously in a drawer, searching for something. Long brown fingers closed over a gilt picture frame, and he pulled it from the drawer. Then he returned to Leslie's side and thrust it into her shaking fingers.

Slowly she glanced down at the photograph of a lovely blonde woman who so resembled herself that for a long moment she was shocked. Of course, on closer examination there were subtle differences. Leslie breathed in deeply. "Marnie?" she managed in a tremulous whisper.

"Yes."

"She's . . . beautiful. . . ."

"Yes," he snapped, grabbing the picture from her and placing it face down on the top of his desk. "Isn't she? As beautiful as poison. Now will you please get out and leave me alone."

The smoldering light in his eyes seared her to the marrow of her bones. The desperate pain she heard in his voice caught at her heart. "Boone, I'm sorry. . . . I-I didn't know. . . ."

"Get out!" he ordered, blind with emotion.

For one long moment her eyes tenderly roamed his handsome features searching for some sign of warmth, but she found none. He was very dear to her, but it was all too clear he cared nothing for her. Even so, she longed to help him, to ease his suffering, but in the end she realized that the only thing she could do to help was leave him. When she went out, the door clicked softly behind her.

As beautiful as poison. . . . Boone's savage utterance lingered in Leslie's mind as she quickly collected her personal belongings in her office. They were strange words from a man who'd been deeply in love with his wife. But then Leslie knew from her own experience after her parents had been killed when their light airplane crashed that anger was a part of grief.

"Leslie, I'd like to talk to you." Rose Mary's gentle voice interrupted.

Startled, Leslie looked up. She wasn't aware that the older woman had come in.

"Haven't you heard?" Leslie began unsteadily. "I've been fired! I'm to leave immediately."

"Not before we have a little talk," Rose Mary pleaded. "I need to explain. . . ."

"Boone already has. He showed me a picture of Marnie. How could you do this without at least warning me?"

"Please . . ."

For the first time Leslie glanced up from her desk and looked at the older woman. Rose Mary's face was filled with warmth and concern as well as a silent plea that Leslie be understanding. In the two weeks that Leslie had known Rose Mary, she'd come to realize that, although Boone's mother could be quite forceful, she was basically a kind-hearted soul.

"All right," Leslie agreed softly. "Why don't you close the door and sit down."

Once seated opposite Leslie, Boone's mother began. "I should have told you from the first, but I was afraid you wouldn't take the job."

"I wouldn't have. . . ."

"As soon as I saw your picture on the application I knew you were the right woman to snap Boone back to life."

". . . because I looked like Marnie. . . ."

"Not only that. There was a vulnerability about you that Marnie never had. Then when I met you in person I saw that you'd suffered yourself, so I thought you might understand what Boone's been going through. And, oh, Leslie, he's suffered so much! Ever since Marnie died . . . he's been different. It's been more than grief! He hasn't had anything to do with women. He seems to hate them all! He's done nothing except bury himself in his work. He's driven himself and the rest of us unmercifully. I've tried everything I knew to bring him out of it, but nothing's worked. . . ."

"And hiring me was still another attempt on your part to help your son."

"Yes. But I was going to explain what I'd done as soon as I saw him."

"You had no way of knowing we would meet by accident."

"No."

"I suppose Boone was desperately in love with Marnie," Leslie coaxed.

"They were childhood sweethearts. They married young, and at first they were very happy. But later, I wasn't so sure. Boone wanted children, but Marnie didn't. And I think she found Winter Park a little confining, but perhaps that's no more than an old woman's imagination. . . . It was just that that last year she seemed so restless and temperamental. I never did seem to be able to stay on the right side of her. But then when she died, Boone carried on so. Yes, I think he loved her very much. That's the only way to explain the way he's been since her death. . . ." Her voice trailed off.

"Rose Mary, I'm afraid your little scheme has backfired. Boone and I met, and . . . things ended disastrously."

"What happened?"

"Don't ask. Suffice it to say that he doesn't like me at all."

"I don't believe that," Rose Mary stated firmly. "He's angry. But he doesn't dislike you. In the year since Marnie died, I've never seen him show any emotion until I saw him this morning . . . with you. You've had an effect on him, no one else has. He cares . . ."

"Not in the right way."

"I'm not sure that's true. Don't leave Winter Park. I promise you that with your qualifications I can easily find you another job by this afternoon. I know you gave up your teaching position to come here. It's the least I could do."

"Rose Mary," Leslie gently refused, "I can't be a part of your scheme, however well-intentioned it may be."

"Well, dear, if you reconsider, you know where to find me."

Later that afternoon Leslie wondered if she'd been too hasty in rejecting Rose Mary's offer to find her another job. Tim's child-support check hadn't arrived yet, and her checking account balance was very low. A move back to Texas was more than she could afford. Besides that she'd signed a lease for her condominium, and she'd lose a substantial deposit.

At two o'clock Karen's teacher called and informed her that Karen was sick, so Leslie rushed up to the school to pick her up. Karen managed only a wan smile at the sight of her mother, and Leslie realized she must be quite sick. Usually Karen bubbled at everything. The child's blue eyes were lusterless, her chestnut curls matted damply to her forehead. When Leslie took Karen's hand to lead her to the car, it was limp and feverish.

Leslie drove at once to Dr. Rome's office, which was ten miles away in a neighboring town. The road was packed with snow, and she had to drive slowly.

Dr. Rome was one of the few doctors in a sixty-mile radius, and as a result his office was jammed. It was nearly six o'clock before she wearily led Karen up the stairs to their condominium. As she held on to Karen with one hand and fumbled in her purse with the other for her keys, she heard the phone inside ringing furiously.

When she at last got inside and rushed to answer it, she knew that the deep, angry tone could belong to only one man. The sound of Boone's voice vibrated through her. "Where the hell have you been?"

Leslie's nerves were stretched ragged with concern for Karen. She hadn't managed to get to the drugstore before it closed for the medicine Dr. Rome had prescribed, and she didn't know what she was going to do. Boone's anger was the final, unbearable assault on her nervous system, and she broke down.

"Mr. Dexter, you are one person I certainly don't have to answer to." With that she slammed the phone back on the receiver.

"Why were you so mean to Mr. Dexter, Mommy?" Karen managed in a tight voice.

"It's a long story, darling. Right now we need to get you into bed."

Ten minutes later Karen was tucked into her bed and Leslie was reading her a fairy tale. Karen's neatly brushed hair shone in the dim light. Beneath the frilly lace canopy of her bed she looked like a tiny princess herself. Just as the child began to nod sleepily, the doorbell buzzed.

Anxious to answer the door before the sound of it wakened Karen, Leslie quickly tiptoed from the room. Throwing the door open wide, she uttered a quick little cry of dismay.

"Boone!"

He stood before her like a bronzed giant—so close she could have reached out and touched him.

Dark chiseled male features filled her vision. His jaw was hard with suppressed anger, but she was more acutely aware of his virile masculinity than ever. In spite of herself some treacherous female part of her responded to him.

She would have forced the door shut once more, but

he leaned against it. Using his powerful arm as a brace, he easily held it open.

"I seem to have used up my welcome," he jeered, smiling so that his even, white teeth were revealed. The thick sarcasm of his statement coiled about her.

She felt weak, unable to do battle with this powerful man. "You certainly have," she agreed. "Now will you go? I have better things to do than get into another argument with you."

"Do you?" His black eyes roved over the blue silk dress clinging provocatively to her female curves in slow stripping appraisal. "Like what—entertaining your latest conquest?" His deep voice dripped acid.

All the color drained from her face; her luminous eyes widened.

"Why won't you just leave me alone?" she cried wearily, backing away from the door so that he could follow her inside. "Haven't you done enough?"

The sight of her shoulders slumped in defeat made him feel vaguely uncomfortable, but he ignored the twinge of compassion that pierced the hardened shell surrounding his heart. "I need to talk to you," he said grimly.

"I can't talk now." Suddenly she felt very close to tears. She couldn't cope with Boone, not after all that had happened today. "My little girl's sick. And I wasn't able to get her medicine because the drugstore's closed. She's too sick to take out in this weather, and I can't leave her. I don't know what I'm going to do."

He caught the quiet desperation in her voice. "Did you take her to see Dr. Rome?" he asked more gently.

Surprised at the faint note of kindness in his voice, she lifted her shimmering eyes and held his deep, dark gaze. "Yes, but I couldn't get the medicine he prescribed."

"I'll get it for you," he said, deeply aroused by her vulnerability, yet not understanding what motivated him to want to help her.

A feeling of relief washed over her. Being a single parent was difficult, especially at a time like this. Shyly, Leslie flashed him a warm smile of gratitude.

Her tremulous mouth flooded him with an emotion that was inexplicably intense. "I'll need to use your phone," he said gruffly, tearing his gaze from her exquisite face.

All Leslie's attention was on his large, strong hands as he dialed the number—those same hands that had known her intimately and shown her heights of rapture she'd never experienced except in his arms. At the burning memory, she flushed, just as his knowing gaze met hers. Quickly, too quickly, she looked away. His deep voice speaking into the receiver broke the awkward silence between them. "David, this is R.B. I need you to open up as a special favor. It's an emergency. . . ."

When he hung up, he turned to her. "I'll need the prescription. . . ."

She fumbled in her purse and found the crumpled scrap of paper. As she placed it in his hand, his touch burned her with his warmth.

"Leslie . . ." His voice was strangely gentle. "I'll bet you haven't eaten all day, have you?"

"N-no. But I'm all right. Don't bother about me. I'll fix something later."

"I'll bring you something," he stated.

When he was at the door, she said, "You don't need to ring the doorbell when you come back. It might wake Karen." Her eyes held his for an endless moment.

"And . . . Boone . . . I do thank you. I don't know what I would have done . . ."

Very gently he lowered his lips and brushed her forehead briefly in a short, sweet kiss. His palm tenderly cupped her chin. For her the moment was one of breathless magic. Then he left, closing the door very softly behind him.

When he had gone Leslie rushed down the hall to see about Karen. The child lay limply against her pillows, her thick coverlet pushed aside. Her cheeks were bright, and when Leslie touched Karen's forehead, she realized the child was burning with fever. Carefully Leslie slipped a thermometer into Karen's mouth, and when she read it, her worst suspicions were confirmed—104 degrees.

Leslie had already given Karen as much aspirin as she could take for the next couple of hours so she decided that all she could do was give her a cool sponge bath.

Half an hour later she was still sponging Karen off when Boone strode silently into the room.

"How is she?"

"Oh, Boone, she's burning up. I've been doing this for nearly thirty minutes, and she's still as hot as a fire-cracker."

"You take a break," he commanded. "I'll take over. I brought you some fried chicken. You go eat."

"Boone, you don't have to do this. . . ."

His hand closed firmly over hers, the one that held the sponge. She felt his other arm at her waist. "I know."

Meekly she obeyed him, and she did feel better after she'd eaten. When she'd finished and was walking down the hall to check on Karen again, she was surprised by the deep sound of masculine laughter mingling with Karen's curious, chirping voice.

"Gee, Mr. Dexter, you're so nice. Are you the same man my mommy was mean to on the phone?"

"The one and only. But don't be too hard on her. I had it coming." The easiness, the genuine friendliness in his voice didn't belong to the same Boone Dexter that Leslie knew. For a fleeting moment, Leslie felt a pang of something akin to jealousy—and toward her own seven-year-old daughter.

"Feeling better?" Leslie called brightly from the doorway.

"I just gave her her first dose of medicine," Boone said gravely. "I think she'll be like a new little girl in the morning. Now go to sleep, sweetheart."

"But I want you to tell me another story. . . ."

"Not tonight. I'll come back when you're better and tell you one," he soothed.

"Promise?"

"I promise." Then he tucked the sheet gently about her.

In the livingroom Leslie said to him, "Earlier you said you needed to talk to me . . ."

There was a subtle hardening of his smooth, dark countenance, but he returned easily, "It'll keep till the morning." He opened the door. "You've been through enough for one day. Get some rest. I'll come back tomorrow . . . around nine."

The sunshine was brilliant on the newly fallen snow the next morning. The cloudless sky was a rich cobalt blue.

Leslie was again wearing her flame silk scarf and her flame silk blouse, accented with her delicate golden chain. Only this time she'd dressed more casually in skintight designer jeans that showed her figure off to enticing perfection.

Apprehensively she searched for things around the house to do to keep her occupied before Boone's arrival. But in a small condominium that was already immaculate, she found herself repeating the same tasks. She was adjusting the coffee table for the third time when she heard Boone's footsteps on the stairs outside. After his crisp knock she forced herself to wait at least half a minute before answering it.

The ruggedly handsome man who stood in the doorway was the same embittered person who'd resoundingly fired her yesterday, and he was again a dark and forbidding stranger. She was acutely aware of his black gaze traveling over her and lingering where her golden chain dangled between her breasts, of his jaw tightening slightly as though something about her appearance disturbed him.

"Come in," she said weakly, wishing she could will her fluttering heartbeats to settle down, wishing he didn't have this strangely powerful pull over her emotions. "Would you like some coffee? I made it especially because you . . ."

His terse words interrupted her. "I've had some."

"Oh." His coldness hurt, but she determined that she would conceal her feelings from him. "Then you don't mind if I pour myself a cup?" she said coolly.

"Not at all." With studied politeness he used her same turn of phrase. "And *you don't mind* if I sit down?"

"Make yourself comfortable," she tossed, "and I'll join you in a minute."

From the kitchen bar she achingly observed the indolent movements of his hard, male frame as he seated himself, sprawling with a casual air across the couch. Because she was thus distracted she spilled some boiling coffee onto her shaking fingers.

"Ouch!" She jerked her hand to her lips, and the cup clattered precariously in its saucer.

"You all right?" Boone called sharply, leaning forward, his great body tense.

For the briefest instant she saw concern flicker in the black depths of his eyes.

"Yes."

Once more his gaze was cool and hard, his tone indifferent. "I'm beginning to think you're accident prone."

After running cool tap water over her fingers, she joined him on the couch. Attempting to regain her composure, she said, "Karen's much better. I want to thank you again."

"Don't bother. Anyone else would have done the same thing." Casually he dismissed his kindness of the night before. "Let's get down to the business at hand."

"By all means." Her voice was as cool as his own. "And what might that be?"

"Yesterday you left me in a damned awkward position, as I'm sure you know."

"I left you? You fired me, remember?"

"You failed to mention your contract with Mr. Carson. When you didn't show up for your appointment . . ."

His cold, steely look made her tremble slightly, but she managed frigidly, "I had no choice in the matter."

"You could have said something. Instead Mr. Carson arrived and you weren't there. He was very upset, needless to say, that you weren't. It took us a while to locate the earnest money contract on the four condominium units he wants to buy. He's also interested in another piece of property. But he kept demanding to know why you weren't there yourself. He said he wouldn't consider using another agent on the deal."

"I'm sorry that Mr. Carson's involved, of course," she retorted icily. "But, Boone, I can't see how any of this is my problem. It's yours. Now I have other things to do that are more important than . . ."

She would have risen, but his brown hand clamped around her tiny wrist like a vise, forcing her to remain where she was. She gasped at his casual touch. A low, unwanted fire simmered in her veins.

"Than a million-dollar deal. I can't imagine what they might be," he said sarcastically.

Neither could she, but she wasn't about to admit this truth. She pulled her fingers free from his.

"Besides," he continued. "It's your sale. You deserve the commission."

She wanted to hurl back the words that she didn't need his money, but that simply wasn't true. She desperately needed it. Having spent all her reserve cash to make this move to Colorado, she needed a lot more than one commission. Tim's late child-support check made her realize more strongly than ever that she was completely on her own. She'd taken the job with his company in good faith. How could she have known that Mrs. Dexter didn't have the authority to hire for the family-run business?

Karen's illness underscored the fact to Leslie that she was a single parent with a child to support. She had too much at stake to allow herself to be treated unfairly. And for whatever reasons, Boone Dexter had fired her unfairly.

"As I understand it," she began slowly, feeling her way, "even though I'm still fired, you want me to come back and handle Mr. Carson's sale. I take my commission, and then it's goodbye."

"That's it," he said blandly, superbly confident that no one in their right mind would pass up such a juicy commission.

"Well, I won't do it!" She took intense satisfaction in the look of stunned shock that swept the placid look from his features.

"You what?" he muttered fiercely.

"You heard me! I won't do it! I don't work for you anymore. I never did. As you so bluntly put it yesterday, my contract with R.B. Dexter isn't worth the paper it's written on without your signature. And if you're thinking of patching up your deal with Mr. Carson, I think I'll give him a call at his hotel and cry on his shoulder. He has a daughter my age who's divorced and struggling to support three children. He won't think too highly of your professional ethics, Mr. Dexter."

" 'Mr. Dexter!' You and I are too intimately acquainted to address one another with last names. And I don't give a damn about professional ethics," he lashed out at her.

"I'd be the first one to agree with you on that score," she managed to retort sweetly.

"What do you want—revenge? More money?"

"Neither of those. The answer's much simpler than that. I want my job. That's all! Your signature on my contract!"

A falling feather could have been heard in the thick, hostile silence.

"That's blackmail!" he uttered savagely.

"Call it what you like," came her faint, yet defiant whisper. "Those are my terms. Take them or leave them."

Trembling, she rose, taking her coffee cup with her and heading for the bar for a refill. But he was right behind her. The coffee cup was wrenched from her fingers and set on the bar. Then he pulled her into his arms, against the muscular sweep of his heated length.

"You little fool! There's no way we can work together!"

Her heart beat against her ribs like a caged, wild thing as she struggled to break free. She felt the rippling muscles of his arms tightly wrapped around her. He held her so fiercely that she could scarcely catch her breath. Blackness whirled around her, and all the hot, angry words that had gone before were momentarily forgotten. She was aware only of the hard contours of his masculinity molded against her yielding curves.

Suddenly something melted in both of them. The sweet, fragile scent of her, the feel of her soft flesh crushed against himself thawed the raging heat of his anger. Vengeance no longer drove him. In its place was raw, hungry desire. And for her, as always, his touch was wonderful madness. Sensual longing flared through them —more intense than ever before—because they'd already had each other once and knew what rapture each could give the other. In spite of everything he'd said to deny it, when he held her in his arms his body told her what he could not admit—that their coming together was the mating of two souls each of whom had spent a lifetime searching for the other.

When his lips claimed hers with bruising pressure she surrendered herself to the mastery of his embrace. Boone drew her onto her tiptoes and bent his head to fervently nuzzle the warm hollow between her breasts. "That damned chain," he muttered thickly, tickling her sensitive flesh with his lips as his mouth traveled over the delicate strand of gold that lay against her breasts. "It's been driving me wild ever since I got here. Did you wear it just to torment me?" There was a time of silence as they kissed one another passionately. "How am I ever going to get you out of my system," he groaned at last as though in pain.

His words made her feel very unwanted, and she was reminded of his true feelings. He didn't really want her. And no matter how she felt, she wasn't going to make the same mistake she had Saturday night. Wrenching herself free, she stumbled blindly away and ran behind the kitchen bar, feeling safer only when something substantial was between them. She stared dazedly out the window at a patch of brilliant snow because she couldn't risk looking at him. She was too vulnerable to his rawly virile, handsome charm. Hugging her arms tightly about her to assuage the empty ache in her heart, she drew a quick, shallow breath.

"Leslie . . ."

"What was that?" She forced a sharpness into her voice that she didn't feel. "Your brand of sexual harrassment? If we're going to work together, you'll have to keep your distance."

His jawline hardened, and she knew that her barb had found its mark. "And that's exactly why you and I can never work together," he hurled back.

"Surely, Mr. Dexter, you have some self-control."

"Not where you're concerned. What does it take to convince you? This?"

He moved toward her with the swift fluid grace of a panther lunging for its prey and pulled her once more into his arms. There was a savage glint in his black flashing eyes, a cruel twist to his sensual mouth, and she quivered with fear. She didn't know this tall dark stranger who held her with such force against his powerful body that she could scarcely draw a breath.

She panted an infuriated, "Let me go," and vainly attempted to struggle free. He caught her by the wrists and pinned them behind her back so that her breasts were mashed flat against his chest. The edge of the bar cut painfully into her hips.

"You see what you do to me," he muttered brutally.

Of course this was just an underhanded trick to make her change her mind, she tried to tell herself. He was deliberately humiliating her. Still she couldn't stop the single tear that spilled over her long lashes and glistened on her cheek.

"Boone, you're hurting me," she gasped. "Surely you don't intend to use force to convince me that we can't work together?" she pleaded.

Cursing softly, he pushed her from him. Suddenly from the hall came Karen's sleepy voice. "I thought I heard voices. Is Mommy being mean to you again, Mr. Dexter?"

Boone turned toward the child in the fluffy white nightgown. For a long moment he hesitated. Then Karen spoke again, filling the uneasy silence with her lilting voice. "I'm sorry Mommy doesn't like you, but she's really very nice once you get to know her."

A faint gentle smile curved his lips. "I'm glad to see you're feeling better, Karen."

"Did you come back to read me a story?"

"Not this time, sweetheart. But I haven't forgotten. Right now I've got to go to work."

He left without once glancing in Leslie's direction, but an hour later when the phone rang Leslie sensed it would be him even before she lifted the receiver from the hook.

"I just signed your contract," he said. "Be in the office by eight tomorrow." He spoke in low measured tones. "But I'm warning you, keep out of my way."

"That will be my pleasure," she returned pertly. A tiny smile of triumph lifted the edges of her lovely mouth as she hung up the phone. She had the impression that rarely did anyone get the best of Boone Dexter and that this was doubtless a unique experience for him.

But her feeling of triumph was fleeting. At the thought of tomorrow a curious dread began to build in her. She'd won the first battle. Nevertheless, she couldn't help wondering who would win the war.

5

_____

The next morning Leslie dressed carefully in a soft, sheer, sea green dress. Every time she moved, the dress swirled and clung to the voluptuous curves of her body. Around her neck hung the delicate strand of gold that had so tantalized Boone the day before. Only today it lay gleaming against the bodice of her silken dress instead of against her own creamy flesh. For the sake of practicality she wrapped herself in a thick silvery hooded fur coat. It was, of course, a synthetic, but it was such an exquisite facsimile that most people assumed it was mink.

There was a hushed stillness when she opened the outer office door. Leslie registered at once that Boone hadn't told anyone she would be coming back to work. Rose Mary and Tad greeted her warmly after they recovered from their surprise, but Boone's door was closed. Leslie was about to walk past it and go into her own office, when she thought better of the idea. It would never do to take Boone's word that he'd signed the contract. She'd better collect it from him herself before doing anything else.

With a boldness she was far from feeling, she knocked on his door.

"Come in," came the deep, masculine voice that was so achingly familiar. Just the sound of it made her toes curl in the impractical, sexy high heels she'd worn. Drawing a quick, shaky breath she forced herself to march briskly inside.

Excitement at the prospect of seeing Boone brought a rosy blush to her cheeks. Her silvery hood had fallen away, and her thick mass of golden tresses framed her face enchantingly. For the briefest moment his eyes flickered over her lovely features, and they were avid with a hungry emotion he at once sought to suppress.

A tiny thrill of feminine triumph coursed through Leslie. At least he was no more immune to her efforts to look attractive than she was to his compelling virility.

"You!" He muttered a savage oath which she only half heard. "I thought I told you to stay out of my way." He slammed the ledger he'd been working on closed.

"So you did," she whispered silkily across the distance that separated them. "But before I go to work, I'd like a copy of my contract—the one with your signature on it. I want to take it to a lawyer . . ."

"A lawyer! Damn! I told you, you have your job back. I have no intention of going back on my word." His glittering black eyes were darkly menacing, the cold, tight line of his mouth ruthless.

"But I can't be sure of that, can I?" she managed to retort, intimidated by his harsh expression.

The contract was under his fingertips, and he lifted it from his desk. "Come and get it then, if you want it," he jeered in a coldly slicing voice. When she reached for it, his hands closed around her wrist. "Not so fast." Anger and some other emotion vibrated in his thick tone. The savage passion she had so effortlessly provoked told her plainly how deeply her mere presence could upset him. "I've given you what you wanted. Now it's up to you to uphold your part of the bargain. Stay out of my way!"

"All right, Boone, I will," she said quietly. "I would never have forced you to give me my job back if I didn't need it desperately. Working around you won't be any easier for me than it is for you."

He released her abruptly, but not before she saw an odd look of pain scrawled across his handsome features.

What she'd said was true. Her feelings for him had been inexplicably intense from the first moment she'd seen him. Where he was concerned she couldn't seem to help herself. She was hopelessly involved with a man who cared nothing for her.

In the weeks that followed Leslie saw little of Boone even though they worked in the same branch office. He was frequently away in Denver or in meetings with the City Council. She wondered if these numerous absences were a deliberate effort on his part to avoid her. As it was too cold for construction, he spent his time planning and coordinating future projects.

Leslie spent her time showing properties. Many of her clients were Mexicans and Texans. Her fluent command of the Spanish language helped her make several sales, and the fact that she was originally from Texas established an instant rapport with the many Texans who loved to vacation in Colorado.

Boone's continued coldness made Leslie nervous, and she was less patient with Karen during the evenings. One night Karen lashed out, "I wish you were still married to my daddy! You never screamed at me then!" After that Leslie struggled to be more even-tempered with her child, but she was not always successful.

During the Thanksgiving holidays Karen flew to Austin to be with her father, and Leslie spent a lonely four days mostly by herself. Since her divorce, holidays had been especially difficult. Leslie ate turkey dinner with her next-door neighbor, Gini, and her family. Tad and his girlfriend Lucy took her skiing Saturday afternoon. The rest of the long weekend she was alone, and never had solitude weighed more heavily on her hands. She thought of Boone and wished that they could start over. But, of course, that was impossible.

Tim was to have Karen again during the Christmas holidays. The evening before Karen was to leave for Texas, Boone called. Thinking it might be her father, Karen answered the phone. Leslie heard Karen's voice piping exuberantly. "Wow, you didn't forget after all, Mr. Dexter. No, tomorrow I'm going to see my daddy for two weeks. You'll have to come tonight. Sure . . . come over any time you like."

A tiny shiver of excitement coursed through Leslie. Boone was coming to see her. Why?

When that question was put to Karen, the child's answer was instantaneous. "To tell *me* a story like he promised when I was sick!"

Both females went to their respective rooms to ready themselves for Boone's imminent arrival. Long cascading curls gleamed as their hair fell over their shoulders. Both wore jeans and velour tops.

When he knocked, Karen ran to the door and threw it open. "Mr. Dexter, come in."

Boone stepped inside, filling the small living room with his masculine presence. A wild shock of pure pleasure ran through Leslie's body at the sight of him. He was so tall and commanding. He wore a navy western shirt that was unbuttoned at the throat. Blue jeans molded his narrow hips. She caught the intoxicating scent of his aftershave. His aura of male virility was so powerful that he completely dominated his surroundings, not only Leslie but also the tiny female reaching gaily up for the red beribboned package he was holding.

Leslie's senses swam, and she sank weakly against the back of a nearby chair for support. Boone raked his eyes over her with a lingering intensity that shattered the remnants of her composure. Just the way he looked at her was dangerous; he could strip away her defenses until her very soul was bared.

"You feeling all right?" he asked her in the way of a greeting as Karen ripped into the package he'd brought her. "You look a little pale."

Those were the first words he'd spoken to her in nearly two weeks—twelve days to be exact. Leslie's throat went dry, and she ran her tongue across the pearly layer of lipstick, unaware of the erotic message she was sending.

"I'm fine," she murmured shakily. "Karen's so excited that you remembered your promise. It was thoughtful of you to bring her a Christmas present."

"It was the least I could do after waiting so long to keep my promise, wasn't it, sweetheart?"

It didn't make Leslie particularly happy to know that all

of his kindness was for the sake of her daughter and not for her.

"A new doll," Karen squealed. "And two dresses! Oh, thank you, Mr. Dexter. And now will you come to my room and tell me that story?"

"Of course."

For at least an hour Boone sat on the edge of Karen's bed telling her stories. From time to time Leslie heard his deep rich laughter blend with the softer tones of her daughter's voice.

The volume of the television was a low drone, and Leslie was restlessly thumbing through a fashion magazine when Boone at last left Karen alone as she finally dozed off. To Leslie's surprise he did not go at once to the door. Instead he sank into the chair beside her. She noticed that his long muscular frame barely fit the chair. She was startled by the way his dark eyes observed her intently. His nearness was deeply unsettling, and she tossed her magazine onto the coffee table.

"I'm afraid Karen's fallen asleep fully dressed," he said, smiling.

Leslie warmed to the friendliness in his manner. Karen certainly brought out the best in his nature.

"That's all right," Leslie began unsteadily. There was a latent sensuality about him that she found disturbing. Just his nearness made her feel slightly breathless. "I know it meant a lot to Karen that you came over."

"I made her a promise, and I had to keep it." His black eyes lazily touched her mouth. Unnerved, she curled her bottom lip inward and caught it with her teeth, moistening it. Little did she realize how provocative this gesture was.

"Can I get you something?" she asked awkwardly, remembering her role as hostess.

"No, stay where you are." His avid gaze seemed to burn through her. "I haven't told you how pleased I've been with your work," he said. "For a beginner you've done a first-class job of selling."

"Why, thank you." His praise made her unaccountably happy.

"I was wrong to have fired you without even giving you a chance, in spite of the fact that I knew why Mother had hired you."

The lingering dark force of his gaze held her spellbound. Or was it just his apology that made her turn all soft and quivery inside? It took a big man to admit he was wrong.

"Boone, I-I think I understand why you did what you did," she said gently.

"I'm not sure you do." His hot intense stare seemed to strip her bare of the clothes she was wearing, leaving her completely exposed to his ravishing gaze. "It hasn't worked—our avoiding each other. I still want you as much as ever."

Restlessly he moved toward her as though he couldn't bear to be so near her without touching her. The springs of the couch groaned as it received his weight, and she was enfolded in the hard circle of his arms. The warmth of his body against her own, and the fresh clean scent of him working on her reeling senses made it difficult for her to control her tumultuous emotions. She tried to twist away, but he held her to him with gentle force.

"And I still want you," a tiny voice in the depths of her mind cried silently. "Wanting . . . without caring is not enough for me, Boone," she said aloud. "It never will be. Maybe I'm old-fashioned . . ."

"I hardly call a woman who goes to bed with a man the first day she meets him old-fashioned," he commented bitterly.

"How long will it take," she flared, "for me to live down that one mistake?"

"A long long time," he muttered huskily. His mouth was so near hers that she felt his warm breath fan her lips. "Some mistakes are worth repeating," he murmured invitingly.

"Not that one," she rasped. Edging away from him, she replied stiffly, "I think you'd better be going."

"I'm in no mood to spend another night alone, knowing that you're over here alone too."

Had he been as lonely as she? Had he spent his nights thinking of her as she had of him? "Then what are you in the mood for?" she retorted, realizing at once what a slip that question was.

"I'd rather show you than tell you," he replied lazily, crushing her back against the soft couch.

"No, no," she whispered fearfully, trying to get up, but she was pinned beneath him. Every movement brought her into even more disturbing contact with his body. He ignored her words. He kissed her full on the lips, very tenderly; he felt her trembling response as her arms circled his neck.

A hot rush of feeling swept through her like a raging undertow pulling her out into the dangerous depths of his desire. Then she caught herself and fought against the whirling passion that was consuming her. "Let me go," she murmured pleadingly. But he did not obey her. "Please, let me go," she cried softly, weakly struggling against him even though she couldn't control the awakening desires his lovemaking aroused.

"No."

A deep flush bathed her face with glowing heat. His lips gently kissed the warmth of her creamy flesh there before wandering once more to her mouth and claiming it fully in a long, breathless kiss.

"You must!" Leslie gasped, dragging the swollen softness of her mouth from his. "Karen! She's in the other room!"

"She's asleep." His warm mouth was hungrily nuzzling downward into the curve of her throat as he molded her body to his own.

"She could wake up and come in here," Leslie forced herself to insist.

"All right," he said wearily, relenting, removing his mouth from her sensitive skin. "But she's leaving tomorrow night. What excuse will you have then?"

His smoldering gaze locked with her own unwilling one, devastating her self-control, compelling her to need him. Surely, if he touched her again, she would be lost. His eyes, black and deep like the darkest depths of the ocean, lured her to follow him into the raging lovetide of his desire.

"Boone, please don't force me into the kind of relationship I can't handle," she begged softly. "No matter what you think, sex isn't just an appetite with me. It entails love, respect . . . friendship . . ."

"Love," he spat contemptuously. "Respect. . . . Women don't understand the meaning of those words."

His harshness was like a quick savage pain, wounding her soul.

"I can see I'll never be anything to you except a body

79

who can give you physical release when you need it," she began weakly. "Well, that's not enough for me. Just because I went to bed with you the first time I met you, I'll never have your respect. Well, maybe you're right! Maybe I don't deserve it."

Unshed tears moistened her thick, long lashes. Seeing them, his mood softened.

"Leslie, you want too much—more than I have to give," he returned with quiet firmness. "You're complicating what should be a perfectly simple situation between a mature man and woman. All I want is sex. You're a beautiful woman, and I need you . . . physically. I can't deny that, but I don't need love or friendship from any woman. I've a mother and sister to love me as well as the necessary men friends I can hunt and fish with when the mood hits me. You're just like all the rest of your sex. You think that because I desire you, you should have total control over me. That's all love and marriage represent to women—control. Power. Well, I've been controlled and used by the last woman."

"No stereotype could fit every woman in the world," she said, attempting to appeal to his logic.

"In this case it does."

"So you have decided to use women—to satisfy you and nothing more?" Her voice was as smooth and soft as silk.

"Bluntly put . . ."

"But true," she sighed.

"Yes."

"I want more . . ."

Brutally his rough voice interrupted her. "Like every other woman, you want to do the using."

His fierce black eyes ravaged her lovely pale features.

"All I know is that what you're offering isn't enough," she admitted unsteadily. "I couldn't live that way and live with myself."

Boone exhaled a long, deep breath of exasperation, showing her clearly that he believed her statement a pose and not the truth. "Have it your own way, but if you have a change of heart . . ."

"I won't."

"Then I'd better be going," he told her levelly. If he couldn't have her on his terms, he didn't want her at all. The harsh planes of his face seemed chiseled from some dark stone. His eyes were flat and hard.

Though Leslie was deeply hurt by his rejection, she tried not to show it.

"Well, then I'll see you at work tomorrow," she said tightly, rising to show him the door.

"Not if I can help it," he muttered savagely, and then he was gone.

It was all too obvious she was of no interest to him as a person. She was only a sexual object.

Throughout the night her thoughts swirled around Boone. As she lay in her bed aching and alone, she remembered everything he had said.

He was right about one thing. She wanted him as much as he wanted her. They had already been to bed once, and she knew what sexual ecstacy he could rouse her to. No other man had ever appealed to her as he did. In some indefinable way he was special, even though she wasn't to him.

Life was short. Why should she pass up an experience that could be so pleasurable, not only for him but for her as well? Yet, she would be swimming in deeper waters than he; she cared, and he didn't. She loved him.

Perhaps she had from the first minute that she saw him. But she'd already suffered once from her first unwise love. And she had Karen's happiness to consider. She had no intention of rushing blindly into a second disastrous love relationship with no thoughts of the consequences.

Fleetingly Leslie thought back over the past. She and Tim had fallen in love and dated when she was in college and he in his first year of surgery residency. When she'd graduated, they'd married, and she'd helped him in the long years of his residency. They'd loved each other intensely when they were young, but somehow other things had come between them. The disintegration of their marriage had happened slowly. The constant pressure of Tim's training, acute financial worries, and an early pregnancy had all taken their toll. They'd both worked very hard, and suddenly when Tim was an established surgeon and they were on the brink of success, Tim had realized that he'd spent his youth in school and he'd never been young. So in the exuberant company of a bevy of younger women, he'd left Leslie in search of his youth.

Odd, but thinking of Tim brought no pain tonight. There was only one man now capable of hurting her, and that was Boone.

As she lay beneath the thick covers of her bed, she determined that no matter what, she wasn't going to let herself become more deeply involved with Boone than she already was. As tempting as a sexual relationship with him might be, it held more danger and ultimate pain than pleasure, if Boone could never grow to love her. She'd been too hurt in the past by Tim to take the risk of sleeping with Boone again in the hopes that the union of their bodies could bring about the ultimate union of their souls. She knew that if it didn't, and he left her, a part of her would die forever.

And so with her decision firmly made, she fell into a deep long sleep and dreamed of a man who was tall and dark and handsome, the only man whose touch inflamed her, the only man who compelled her love, but a man who refused to make a place for her in his heart.

6

·oeoeoeoeoeoe·

Two days later Leslie was sorting through a stack of papers on her desk. She'd been so busy lately that she hadn't had a chance to do any routine filing or other office work.

"Looks like you're digging out," Tad said warmly from the doorway. "When you finish, why don't you come next door and give me a hand?"

"Hi, Tad. How's it been going?" Leslie smiled at him, tossing her golden hair as she looked up at the handsome young man who'd become a casual friend.

"Not too hot. Lucy's gone home to spend the holidays with her parents, and I'm feeling pretty lonely. She won't be back until New Year's Eve. We have a date for the Devil's Brand Ranch annual party that night."

"Well, at least you have something to look forward to.

I've been feeling pretty lonely myself the last couple of days. Karen's gone too."

"You coming to the office party tonight?"

"I-I hadn't given it a thought," she replied casually, toying with the end of a pencil. That wasn't exactly true. She felt nervous at the idea of driving in snow at night alone, and she hadn't been to a party since her divorce. Boone had been out of the office for the last two days, but Rose Mary had told her he was planning to come to the Christmas party.

"Well, if you decide you want to come, I'd be glad to drive you," he offered gallantly.

"Why, Tad, if you don't mind, I'll accept your offer. The idea of sitting home alone tonight definitely doesn't appeal to me."

"I'll pick you up at seven."

That evening Leslie was darkening her eyebrows with a deft stroke of a pencil when the telephone rang. Picking it up on the third ring, she instantly recognized her exhusband's languid Texan drawl. Fearing the worst, her heart lodged in her throat.

"Tim, is . . . is . . . Karen . . . Is everything all right?"

"She's fine. I mean it's nothing serious."

Leslie sagged with relief against the bar stool.

"What is it then?" she asked.

"She's very upset about our divorce. She wants us to get back together again, or at least to talk to each other."

Leslie gasped. "It's been eighteen months. She's never said anything to me."

"She didn't say anything during Thanksgiving, but last night she cried for hours. She kept saying you'd been fussing at her all the time, and she knows it's because I left you. She said all she wants for Christmas is for me to come up to Colorado and visit you so you'll feel better. She won't even look at any of the Christmas presents I've bought her. I think she secretly hopes that if we see each other again we'll be able to patch things up."

"It's definitely too late for that," Leslie sighed wearily, thinking of all the scars and months of hurt that made a reconciliation impossible.

"I know. But she's only seven. She can't understand. I've decided to fly her back up there myself on the thirty-first. Maybe you could think of some place we could go out New Year's Eve . . . for Karen's sake . . . unless you have other plans."

This was the last thing she needed, but as she thought back over how nervous she'd been with Karen lately, she realized her behavior must have threatened Karen's security. If Tim made the effort to come to Colorado and she refused, Karen might grow resentful toward her.

"I definitely don't have other plans, and I guess if this is important to Karen . . ."

"Good, it's a date. I'll see you on the thirty-first."

"Oh, Tim, what will our going out accomplish?"

"Karen and I'll get a good night's sleep tonight for one thing. Here, I'll let you tell Karen you've agreed to it."

As soon as she hung up, Leslie dialed the Devil's Brand Ranch and made reservations for two for their annual New Year's Eve dance. It would feel strange going out with Tim again; she wasn't looking forward to an evening with him at all. Once she would have given anything for just such an invitation, but now another man claimed her love.

A brief flicker of annoyance at Tim for letting Karen maneuver them into an evening together passed through Leslie's thoughts. Tim had always been lax with Karen, and now that he rarely saw her, he spoiled her totally when he did have her. If he had tried, he could have found a suitable explanation that would have soothed Karen, and they wouldn't be faced with having to spend an evening together.

Slender fingers curled tightly into Tad's coat sleeve as Leslie's long-lashed gaze swept the crowded room and found Boone at once. A swift pain stabbed her heart at the sight of him so elegantly dressed, yet so ruggedly handsome—and at the same time so totally unconcerned whether she appeared tonight or not.

His well-cut gray suit fit his lean body to perfection. Every movement of his powerful frame was as lithe and fluid as a jungle cat's. In spite of his debonair attire, there was a quality of danger about him, of latent virility, that enhanced his attraction to the female sex. Women fluttered around him, laughing and chattering.

Leslie drew a small, shaky breath. Her dry throat ached. Suddenly she realized how much she'd missed just seeing him these past two days.

The pair of striking, look-alike redheads at Boone's side were the second people in the room to catch Leslie's attention. The younger girl was the same one Leslie had seen him with at the warming house the first day she'd met him. It was obvious that they were on intimate terms, and Leslie felt her heart was as thoroughly green as her eyes.

As Tad bent to help Leslie from her coat, Boone's

black gaze swung to her. The instant he saw her, his features hardened. The heat of his anger seemed to shrivel all the happiness in her heart.

Why had she come? Seeing him like this and having him indicate so clearly how much he disliked her was even more painful than having to work in the same office with him. At least during the day she had her work to distract her.

Rock music filled the air as Boone devoured her with his eyes. His lingering gaze swept with possessive force over her body, which was alluringly clad in a long-sleeved, low-cut black gown that hugged her supple curves like an outer silken skin. At her pale throat white sapphires sparkled. The necklace was a gift from her grandmother.

"Would you like a drink?" Tad offered.

"Y-yes, that would be nice." She flashed him an artificially bright smile.

On no account must she ruin Tad's evening because of the way she felt. She was determined to make an attempt, however difficult, to have fun. And she was more successful than she would have dreamed possible. She was constantly the center of a lively crowd when she was not being stolen away to dance. If she laughed a little too frequently or drank a little too much, well, no one seemed to notice.

No one except Boone. His sharp gaze twisted knots in her stomach every time she chanced to look at him.

Josh, a salesman from another branch office, was dancing with her, holding her closer than she would have liked, when a steely voice from over her shoulder demanded rather than asked, "Can I cut in?" A fiery thrill shot down her spine at the sound of those deep, masculine tones.

"Sure, R.B."

Leslie's heart pounded in her throat; startled green eyes met the hard blackness of his compelling gaze as Boone's arms slid possessively around her. She felt the hot pressure of his fingers against the naked flesh of her back, and a delicious shiver traced through her as she allowed her body to melt against his. Three glasses of wine on an empty stomach had gone to her head, and even though she knew she was playing with fire, she deliberately sought to arouse him, to make him ache for her as she ached for him.

Her lips were pressed against his stiff dress shirt; her warm breath seeped through the fabric and made contact with his own hot flesh.

"Have you been dancing with all the men like this?" his hoarse voice demanded against her earlobe.

"No, only you," she murmured, twining her fingers into the thickness of his raven hair that curled over the edge of his starched collar.

She felt his lips in her hair, nuzzling the sensitive flesh near her temple. She went strangely warm.

"Oh, Boone," she sighed.

"There ought to be a law against this," he murmured huskily.

When the music stopped, they remained locked in one another's arms for a long moment as though spellbound. Neither were aware of Rose Mary watching them from afar, a broad, complacent smile dimpling her plump features.

Tad came up to them and said, "Sorry to

interrupt. . . ." An angry flush darkened Boone's face, hardening his expression. "I just wanted to tell Les that my brother called me, and I've got to go now. Josh has agreed to drive Leslie home tonight."

"You can tell Josh I'll drive her myself," Boone contradicted in such a fierce tone that all the tenderness she'd felt while dancing with him was destroyed.

Tad, sensing trouble, quickly excused himself.

"I'd rather go with Josh," Leslie inserted stiffly, afraid of her own emotions and not trusting herself to be alone with Boone.

"You don't have any choice," came Boone's firm reply as he tightened his grip about her waist.

Leslie was deeply offended by his high-handed manner. "I said I'd rather . . ."

"You little fool!" Boone snapped angrily. "Josh has been drinking. It's been snowing all day, and the roads are as slick as glass."

"He looks all right to me," Leslie tossed defiantly and would have moved away had Boone's hard arms not imprisoned her.

To her stunned amazement he rasped, "Marnie died on a night like this. I let her go—in spite of the fact that she'd been drinking."

Boone drove slowly, skillfully maneuvering the Cadillac through the thickly falling snow. The roads were packed with snow; deep drifts were piled on either side of the highway. Boone had insisted on driving Josh home himself, thus, the roads they followed were unfamiliar to her.

When he headed into the garage of a three-story mansion nestled in a thick grove of spruce, she said, "Boone, this isn't where I live . . ."

"I know. It's where I live."

Before she could reply, he was already outside, going around the front of the car to let her out. "You didn't even ask me if I wanted to come here."

"I knew you'd say no."

She let him help her from the car. What was the use of opposing him at this point? It was obvious he had no intention of taking no for an answer.

The interior of his home was as beautiful as the exterior. Sheets of glass spanned one wall. In a glance she saw how completely masculine his house was—unfinished slanting cedar on the walls, burnished gold carpeting, heavy leather furnishings, Indian paintings. Nowhere was there evidence of a woman's softening touch. The house was as completely masculine as the man himself.

He helped her from her coat. Where his fingers grazed the naked warmth of her flesh, excitement tingled faintly. "That's some dress," he said, his gaze roaming over her from head to toe, taking in the feathery curls falling lightly over her shoulders, her brilliant eyes, their color intensified because of the heavier evening makeup she was wearing. But his gaze continued downward to the firm swell of her breasts visible above the decolletage neckline of her gown.

A becoming blush heightened her color. Just the way he looked at her made her feel slightly breathless. Then the carved planes of his face hardened.

"What were you trying to do?" he drawled thickly. "Move in on Tad while Lucy's gone? Or did you just want to make a spectacle of yourself? You had every man at the party drooling after you."

"How dare you accuse me of trying to come between

91

Tad and Lucy! And as for this dress—why every other woman there was wearing a cocktail gown." Leslie hurled the statement at him indignantly, stung by his harsh words.

"You hardly looked like every other woman there. Every man at the party outdid himself on your behalf."

"Who are you to be talking? You spent most of your time with that beautiful redhead. Why, she's young enough to be your daughter!"

"She practically is," he returned, smiling suddenly as his mood unaccountably lightened. "She's my niece. Were you jealous?"

Painfully. . . . But that was scarcely an admission she relished making. Nevertheless, his intent gaze made a lie impossible. "I-I . . ." She looked away, thoroughly disconcerted. "Oh, you're impossibly conceited!"

"I'm willing to admit I didn't like seeing you with Tad." His voice, low and well-modulated, wrapped her in its warmth.

The thought that he actually might care for her more deeply than he chose to admit and was extremely jealous penetrated her senses with the force of lightning, melting away her anger. Vainly she tried to fight off the emotions that he could so effortlessly arouse by adopting a kind manner. She had to keep her wits about her for she was very alone with a man who'd made his intentions terribly clear on more than one occasion.

"He just drove me to the party," she replied coolly. "Tad and I are friends. That's all."

Boone had moved behind the bar and was splashing expensive Scotch over an ice cube in a crystal glass. She watched as he opened the brand of diet cola she always drank at work for her.

"The other night you said that was something you wanted from a man—friendship," Boone persisted, lifting his black eyes to her face.

Her cheeks burned, and she quickly tore her gaze from his. How could his mere look be so disturbing?

"I suppose it is—one of the things," she said tightly.

He moved toward her, his every step one of fluid grace. Again she was intensely aware of his sexuality, of his potent virility. His nearness was so intoxicating that it swept away her fear of the danger.

Her fingers wrapped gratefully around the cola he offered her. For no reason at all her throat suddenly felt very dry. "Thank you," she murmured softly.

His raven hair glinted in the overhead track lights like polished ebony. His dark features seemed to be carved from teak. Her gaze drifted to the sensual curve of his mouth and lingered for a breathless instant. He was unnervingly handsome! She struggled to fight back the erotic memories of that first night when he'd made love to her.

Black fire flamed in his eyes, and she quickly swept her lashes downward, not wishing to read their sensual message. But not before a hot blush painted her cheeks a telling crimson. It was obvious that he was remembering that first night too.

"It's been hell these last two days—without you, Leslie," Boone muttered hoarsely.

"Boone, if you brought me up here because you thought I'd change my mind, you were wrong. I may have had several glasses of wine too many, but I still know what I'm doing."

"I brought you up here because you were so stunningly beautiful tonight I wanted a few minutes alone with you." His gaze touched the golden tumble of hair, the exquisite loveliness of her face.

As her eyes met his, she felt the will to resist him draining from her. If he didn't take her home soon, she would be lost.

"Boone . . ."

"Leslie, I want you enough to try things your way."

Leslie sensed that this was the closest he'd ever come to humbling himself for a woman.

His voice was low and husky; his sincere dark gaze caressed her, eliciting a multitude of confusing emotions. A wild feeling of elation rippled through her. There was an odd catch in her throat as she looked at him. Then she was immediately besieged by doubts. Was this a play to salve her conscience and thereby get her into his bed? No, she knew him well enough from having worked with him that he meant what he said.

"What do you have in mind?" she asked tremulously.

"Could I take you skiing tomorrow? On Saturday the slopes are crowded and with the sub-zero weather and all the clothes we'll be wearing, that should make it easier to keep things on a . . . 'friendship' basis." She caught the bite of harsh self-mockery in his voice.

"You know I don't know how to ski very well," she replied humbly.

His intent gaze ignited a liquid fire that flowed through her arteries. "All you need is practice," he said suavely. "I could give you a few pointers. Besides skiing isn't what matters—it's our getting to know each other that's important."

"Boone . . . I . . ." She was suddenly at a loss for words.

"I want you with me Leslie—even without sex." He

strode to the television set and flicked it on. "How do you feel about a late movie?"

"W-why that would be nice," she said, totally surprised at this suggestion. When she would have sat in a nearby chair, his arm came around her waist.

"Sit with me on the couch." His heady male smile made her heart turn a somersault. His coal-black eyes lingered on her moist lips. The sensual impact of his nearness made Leslie try to pull away, but he caught her to him. "Don't be afraid."

"I'm not afraid," she denied, but even her words trembled.

"Liar," he whispered gently into her hair. "But you're not the only one. . . ." His statement caused her to remember his fierce determination not to ever let any woman close to him again.

He led her to the couch and pulled her down beside him. His arms wrapped around her, and he held her close against him as if she were very dear. But his embrace was affectionate, not sexual.

The nerve ends in her shoulder tingled where it came into contact with his body. Then she forced herself to concentrate on the movie, a comedy, and soon her shaky giggle blended with his own rich, deep laughter.

An hour passed. He held her snuggled against him on the soft couch, his dark brown hands interlocked with her smaller ones. There was an easiness between them that had never existed before.

When the movie was over, Boone switched it off and freshened their drinks. "Perhaps it's time we got to know each other as people," he said, a faintly sardonic expression hardening his chiseled features. "Tell me about yourself."

"Well, you already know that I'm just another 'desperate' divorcee with a child to raise. . . ."

She told him of her childhood and school days, revealing everything except the details about her marriage and divorce. "And now," she said, "it's your turn to tell me about yourself."

"There's not much to tell."

"You're older than I am, and I talked for fifteen minutes," she teased.

"It's the same old story of poor boy makes good."

"No two stories like that are ever the same," she said gently. "Yours is uniquely your own."

"My dad died when I was just a kid. After that I always worked—summers, holidays, even during school. You name it, and I've done it. All my life I wanted to be a doctor, and my last year in college I was lucky enough to get a scholarship. I worked constantly at odd jobs because the scholarship money wasn't nearly enough. Mother had to have several operations during that time, and we never had enough money. We both went without so that I could stay in school. And then I started dating Marnie again. We'd gone together in high school, but this was different. . . ." A shuttered look darkened his features as he remembered.

A tiny twinge of jealousy ripped through Leslie that was quickly followed by guilt.

Boone's deep voice continued. "I spent so much time with Marnie my grades fell. I never had enough time to study because she and I were constantly together. It wasn't really her fault. When she got pregnant, I dropped out of school and married her. A month later she lost the child, and although for a few years I talked of going back to school, I never did. I had a wife to support, and Mother needed my help. So I determined to make it any way I could. Somehow I ended up in construction and real estate. You can guess the rest."

Leslie caught the thread of fierce determination and struggle that lay behind his success. He was a man who stopped at nothing to get what he wanted, a man who could turn failure into success.

He'd told her about himself, but she was sure that there were great gaps in his story. She was no closer to understanding the reasons that lay behind his distrust and bitterness toward women than ever.

Boone did not touch her in any intimate manner during the evening until he drove her home and they stood beneath a shower of golden light in front of the half-opened door to her condominium. Ignoring the tiny quiver of anticipation that shivered through her, she would have darted inside, but he caught her wrist and gently drew her into the hard warmth of his arms.

"Surely friendship isn't all you want from our relationship, Leslie," he mocked, a bold, sardonic grin slashing his features.

"No, Boone, it isn't," she admitted hesitantly.

She felt especially close to him this evening because he'd made such an effort to relate to her as a person instead of someone he merely desired. Even before he leaned down she was stretching onto her tiptoes to meet the deliberate descent of his mouth. The instant flesh met flesh, a moan of pure pleasure escaped her lips.

At the touch of his mouth—hard and firm, yet feather-light against her own—a warm wonderful feeling spread through her, making her pulse trip crazily, making her draw short, irregular breaths. Her fingers, spread like open fans against his shoulders, twined around his neck.

Her mouth parted at the insistent pressure of his, and his tongue slid inside and explored the moist, intimate depths of her mouth. She felt his fingers trace a tingly path down the slender column of her throat to the place where her breast swelled above her low-cut gown. Yet he did not hold her close to his body.

With consummate skill, his lips continued their slow method of arousal until Leslie's need grew into a terrible ache that only he could cure. In everything he did— every movement, every gesture—it was apparent that he was experienced at the art of making love. Even though he vowed he was bitter toward all women, he was an expert when it came to sexual intimacy with them. But Leslie was too consumed with wondrous, passionate feelings to ponder how a man who could give a woman so much pleasure could swear he hated them.

As always his virile magnetism affected her. Hot molten desire surged through her. She felt weak with longing, aflame with wanton, carnal impulses; the thought of him going home to his own bed, of both of them sleeping alone struck her as distinctly depressing. She clung to him, desperately seeking to prolong this treasured moment of shared closeness.

His breathing was as harshly uneven as her own. She felt the pounding of his heart beneath her lips when she kissed the warm flesh of his throat. They were both sensually hungry for more than mere kisses could satisfy. His mouth tugged at the bottom of her earlobe, and she shuddered. She had only to invite him to stay. . . .

Yet she knew that she couldn't sleep with him again when there was no commitment between them, when he thought no more of her than any woman he would use for his pleasure.

He was the first to pull away. A tiny cry was wrenched from her throat. But as she gazed up into the dark handsomeness of his face, the words, "Don't go," didn't come.

A calloused finger reached up and gently fondled a mussed strand of gold that had fallen into her eyes. Her eyes met his own, which were deep and dark with desire. Her lips still trembled from his kisses.

"Good night, Leslie." His low voice was rough with controlled emotion. "I hope you get more sleep than I will."

"I'll see you in the morning, Boone," she said huskily.

As she closed the door softly behind her, a tiny rapturous smile illuminated her features until she was truly beautiful as she anticipated the day that was to follow.

7

A tiny quiver of disappointment caught in Leslie's throat as Boone's words penetrated her senses.

"I hope you don't mind if Dina and Tess go with us?" Easily he slid Leslie's skis onto his broad shoulders. His white smile made her go weak with happiness, dispelling her doubts.

"Dina and Tess?" she questioned tentatively.

"Those two beautiful redheads I was paying so much attention to last night." A devilish glint danced in his black eyes.

His deep chuckle intensified her warm happy feeling. It was so good to be with him again that she didn't care if she had to share him with his sister and niece.

As soon as they reached the Cadillac, Boone helped Leslie into the plush leather interior of the front seat and made the necessary introductions. Dina was the elder of the two; Tess was the vivacious beauty Leslie had first seen him with. Dina was friendly at once, but Tess barely managed a sulky smile in Leslie's direction.

Snow crunched under the tires as Boone maneuvered the car onto the main road. As they sped to the ski slope, conversation flowed around Leslie. Boone was a different person with his sister and niece. He was no longer dark and forbidding. Leslie marveled at how changed he was, and as she listened to the light banter between brother and sister, she learned things about him she could never have learned otherwise. Dina was as chatty and open as he could be secretive. Tess, however, entered the conversation only when courtesy compelled her to, and Leslie grew apprehensive that she might somehow be the cause of Tess's bad mood.

Conditions for skiing were perfect. The deep snow-packed slopes were topped with ten inches of soft powder. Boone chose Leslie to be his partner riding the lifts, and as they were whisked over the snow-covered trees, they looked in wonder at the silent, agile dance of the skiers as they whisked by beneath them.

The day was gloriously beautiful. Or perhaps Leslie only thought so because she was with Boone and for once there was a rare sense of harmony between them. Deep blue skies against gleaming white mountains stretched into the distance for as far as they could see. The frigid air stung her cheeks, and she snuggled close to Boone.

Boone pointed toward a ragged mountain. "That's Snowpeak over there. This spring I'll begin developing it into another ski area. We'll start by clearing some runs and building the lifts as well as a base lodge and a second lodge halfway up the mountain."

"Sounds exciting," Leslie murmured contentedly, reveling in the joy of simply being with him.

"I've got a lot of my own money tied up in that project," he continued.

"But are there enough hotel rooms and condos in Winter Park to house more skiers?" she asked.

"No. But then that's the kind of problem a builder likes." His bold smile devastated her senses, and for a moment she completely lost track of what he was saying and concentrated on the sensual line of his lips. "For the past week I've been with my architect going over plans for several more condominium units."

Boone continued talking and Leslie listened. She was aware of his arm wrapped lightly around her possessively, of his body pressed close to hers. This time of sharing, of talking to one another was intensely precious to her. She could almost forget the hostility that had come between them. For Boone, being with her, telling her of his plans and his dreams, was stimulating. He hadn't enjoyed himself so much in months, no, years.

The hours passed too swiftly because they were both so happy. The day was one of deep contentment for both of them. Leslie found herself enjoying riding the lifts with Boone far more than she did the sport of skiing itself; only then did she have him all to herself.

It was nearly four o'clock. Leslie's cheeks were bright from the cold. Her fingers felt numb in her thick gloves, and she clapped them together as one of her instructors had advised to improve the circulation. Leslie, Boone, and the two redheads were at the top of the mountain when Dina said to Boone, "Tess said she'd ski down with

Leslie if you wanted to race me down a couple of Black Slopes."

Boone's eyes flashed with enthusiasm, and Leslie knew that he wanted to accept his sister's challenge to go down the Black Slopes, which were the expert runs. They'd grown up skiing the mountains, and they both relished the thought of a quick run to the bottom.

"Go ahead, Boone," Leslie said softly. "I'll be all right."

"You're sure?"

The genuine concern for her that lit the black depths of his eyes made the sacrifice of his company more than worth it.

"Yes."

Her face was radiant as he bent his lips and brushed her forehead gently. Both were unaware of Tess observing them, hostility etched into the downward droop of her mouth and a deep frown ravaging the loveliness of her young face.

From behind them came Dina's exuberant, "On your mark, get set, go!"

Reluctantly, Boone dragged his lips from Leslie's smooth skin. But his eyes lingered caressingly on her for a long moment.

"You'd better hurry," she chided gently, not wanting him to go at all.

"I always give her a minute head start," he explained. "This time I'll give her two minutes."

But all too soon two minutes were up and he was gone. She was left alone on the vast stillness of the mountain with only the sullen Tess for company.

Leslie turned and saw that Tess was glaring at her with a look of utter hatred contorting her expression. Leslie asked the younger girl lightly, in a vain attempt to dispel her dark mood, "Do you want to go first, or should I?"

"Suit yourself," Tess said in a seething, low tone.

Such blatant hostility could not be ignored.

"Have I done something to make you mad?" Leslie asked gently. "If I did, I'm sorry. Maybe if you'd tell me . . ."

Hazel eyes glimmered darkly with rage. "You're just like *she* was!" Tess lashed savagely, spoiling the beautiful moment that had passed between Leslie and Boone a moment before. The harshness of her tone shattered Leslie's euphoria completely. "You may have Boone fooled. But not me! I can see right through you. You don't care for him—not really!"

"I do care for him. I'm sorry if . . ."

"Well, he doesn't care for you! And he never will! It's her! Only her! He wants her, but she's dead! He's only interested in you because you remind him of her! Can't you see that?"

All the blood seemed to drain out of Leslie's features as though the blow she had received were physical rather than emotional. Pain clogged her throat. She could scarcely speak. "That's not true!" she managed in a tight whisper. "That's not true!" But even as she denied it, the doubt had been solidly planted in her heart.

Tess turned then and said, "I suppose you should ski first. I promised Boone I'd see you down the mountain."

Woodenly Leslie turned her skis so that they pointed straight downward. The tears that formed in her eyes but did not fall blurred her vision, but she sped down the mountain recklessly.

She was nearly to the bottom before she recovered

herself at all. Only when she saw Boone scanning the mountain side for her did she slow her pace. He would be upset if she took risks; if she fell he would blame himself for not having skied with her.

Leslie paused on the sheer side of the slope. Boone would think she was resting. But she was really trying to compose herself before she skied to the bottom so that she could face him without him immediately realizing that something was wrong.

Tess skied past her, her long skis slicing into the snow like sabers, a shower of powder flying on either side of her graceful form. Leslie watched her without malice even though Tess had deliberately lashed out at her to upset her.

The younger girl clearly loved Boone very much, and everything she'd said had been to protect him. All the females in his life certainly took it upon themselves to look after Boone's best interests, Leslie thought ruefully. First Rose Mary had hired her because she looked like Marnie. And now his niece had attacked her for the very same reason.

Leslie wasn't ready to ask Boone what the basis of his attraction was for her. The bond between them was too tenuous. Leslie knew too well that Marnie was a dangerous subject. The first day he'd met Leslie he'd warned her not to ask him about his wife, that she belonged to a closed chapter in his life. Later when he'd been making love to her, he'd called out her name. What did it all mean? Was she really only a look-alike substitute for his wife? Or was he beginning to care something for her?

But these questions would have to remain unanswered for the time being because she sensed it was more important to develop her own relationship with Boone. No matter how desperately she wanted answers, she would have to wait until the time was right.

Boone and Leslie were in the warming house drinking hot tea. Dina and Tess had excused themselves to go down to the locker room.

"Something's wrong," Boone said astutely, his knowing eyes examining her pale features. "What happened up there on the mountain? Did you get scared?"

"You might say that," she hedged. "But I'm all right. I'm just a little cold. That's all."

"Here." Boone nestled her more closely against his side. "Drink your tea."

When Tess and Dina returned, Leslie caught the flicker of irritation that flared in Tess's tawny eyes at the sight of Boone holding her tightly, and all her doubts returned, obliterating whatever joy his nearness produced.

That night when he invited her out to dinner she pleaded a headache, and he reluctantly acceded to her wishes. Then she was alone with only her doubts for company.

Boone was away for the whole of the next day, and her only contact with him was a phone call late in the afternoon at which time he invited her for dinner the following evening. Readily she accepted.

The doorbell buzzed twice the next night before Leslie rushed, hair brush in hand, to answer it. Breathlessly she flung the door open wide, and her face instantly lit with pleasure at the sight of Boone towering before her, strong and masterful as though he were a granite statue instead of the vital man he was. Then he smiled down at her, and as always she felt devastated by his sensual power, by the sheer force of his male charisma.

"I'm sorry it took me so long to get to the door," she said.

"It was worth the wait," his deep voice admired. His gaze roamed her curves lusciously displayed in clinging red silk. The warmth in his eyes took her breath away and caused her heart to flutter wildly. When he deliberately sought to charm, he was overpoweringly able to do so.

"I'm not quite ready," she said, stating the obvious. Her stockinged feet were bare of shoes. Her golden hair tumbled in becoming disorder. "Come inside while I finish dressing."

"You don't have to on my account," his amused voice teased.

Something in his tone made her knees go traitorously weak. Her stomach felt jittery.

"Let me help you with that zipper," he offered.

She'd forgotten completely that she'd only managed to zip it halfway up her back. Before she could slip from his grasp, she quivered with shock as his cold hands brushed the warmth of her flesh.

"Boone," she struggled, wanting to escape him for fear he would sense how much even his casual touch could arouse her, "your hands are cold . . ."

"You know what they say. 'Cold hands, warm heart,'" his low, husky voice mocked. "And tonight that old cliche definitely rings true." She tried to ignore the disturbing effect his words had on her, but was not wholly successful. "Leslie, it's only been a day, but I've missed you," he murmured.

His hands moved through her hair in a caressing

motion, lifting up the heavy, billowing tresses. She felt
the hot, moist pressure of his lips graze a tender place at
the nape of her neck, and she shivered. "I missed you
too, Boone."

If they were going to make it to dinner they'd better
leave quickly, she thought, sensing that he had an intense
desire for her tonight and realizing that she felt the same
way. Her only chance was to remove herself to her room
and get ready, thereby escaping the magnetic range
of his personality that overpowered her will to resist
him.

Twisting free from his embrace, she asked, "Could I fix
you a drink?"

"If I can't have you, I guess I'll have to settle for one."
His warm gaze and sexual innuendo made her heart beat
more quickly. "But I can make it myself. You go on and
get ready before I forget why in the hell we're going
out . . . when staying in makes so much more
sense. . . ."

Boone drove her to a French restaurant tucked against
the side of a mountain that commanded a magnificent
view of a moonlit valley. After the haughty maitre d'
seated them beside a window that looked out upon the
wintry fairyland beneath, he struck a match, and candle-
light glimmered from a crystal and silver hurricane lamp
in the center of an elegantly set table. Fine bone China
shone on white linen.

Leslie was unaware of how lovely she was. In the soft
golden light her hair shone like cornsilk; her smooth skin
glowed. She felt the warmth of Boone's gaze drifting over
her, intimately touching the straight, delicate bone struc-
ture of her nose, the moistened curve of her lips, and the
pale column of her throat. For a long moment his eyes

lingered where the upward tilt of her breasts thrust against the red silk.

A rush of warmth brought a rosy hue to Leslie's cheeks as a stiff cardboard menu was placed between her trembling fingers, and she dragged her eyes from his own boldly dark ones. Vainly she tried to concentrate on the menu in an attempt to still the confusing sensations his look aroused.

He was seducing her with his eyes, yet little did she know how she affected him. The drowsy, voluptuous, yielding expression on her own face inflamed him. The gentle smile of her full red lips invited him to plunder their softness. Her involuntary blush told him that she read the sensual message of his own magnificent dark eyes and responded to it.

He reached across the table and took her slender hand in his own large dark one. His calloused thumb stroked her soft palm in a slow, circular motion that was acutely disturbing. Her eyes met his for an endless moment, and the blazing passion she saw in their ebony depths jolted through her, kindling a similar emotion in her that she sought desperately to suppress.

Wildfire raced through her arteries as a primitive pagan song quickened the tempo of her pulse. Wanton memories of the rapture she'd known when he'd made love to her assailed her. She wanted him again—desperately. Her hand squeezed his very tightly in an unconscious effort to fuse her flesh to his.

Then, quickly as though burned, she drew her hand from his to escape the heady erotic stimulation of his flesh moving in a slow, stroking motion against hers.

Nervously, she bit her bottom lip, hoping the pain of this action would bring her to her senses.

"You shouldn't have brought me to such an expensive place," she said unsteadily, trying to break the sexual tension between them.

"How do you know it's expensive?" His low tone flowed around her like sensual music. There aren't any prices on the menu." There was a smile in his deep voice. Again his heated gaze slid over her, causing a strange warmth to course through her.

Violins began to play softly, and the romantic melody only served to increase Leslie's vulnerability to the potent charisma of the virile man who sat opposite her.

Dinner was superb: onion soup gratinée, watercress and tomato salad, sliced filet mignon with marrow and truffles, ratatouille, and macedoine of fruit. Every luscious bite seemed to melt in Leslie's mouth, and she forced herself to eat slowly, to prolong the meal.

"You've toyed with that last strawberry for at least fifteen minutes," Boone drawled pleasantly as he sipped his brandy from a crystal liqueur glass. "If you aren't going to eat it, feed it to me."

There was something almost sexual in his husky invitation. Her long lashes fluttered in confusion as she stabbed the strawberry with her fork and proceeded to do as he had asked. All evening she'd avoided looking at him, but now her gaze swept hesitantly to the bronzed handsomeness of his face. For no reason at all her heart beat in an oddly pained rush and her fingers trembled. Carefully she inserted the berry between his lips. When she removed the fork, he munched into the juicy fruit.

"That was good." His black eyes held hers. "Your hand is shaking," he said at last. "Why?"

"B-because . . ."

"Cold?" he murmured.

"A little," she lied.

"Then why don't we dance." Already he was rising from his chair and coming around to help her from hers.

His arms wrapped around her, and he drew her body close against his. The swaying motion of their bodies undulating rhythmically together to the soft sensuous violin music stimulated every sense in her body. She was aware of every place he touched her; of the light pressure of his hand at her waist, of his other hand curling her fingers against the hard warmth of his shoulder, of his lips buried in the masses of her hair, of his breath fanning the wayward tendrils of gold at her temple.

All the strength drained from her, and she melted against him, clinging to his hard strength for support. His every movement was expert, and as they slowly swirled in one another's arms all of her remaining will to resist him flowed out of her.

Being with him was the most natural thing in the world; it seemed to her that her loving him was preordained.

From somewhere in the depths of Leslie's mind, Tess's words returned to haunt her. "He doesn't care for you . . . and he never will! It's her! Only her! He wants her, but she's dead! He's only interested in you because you remind him of her. . . ."

Perhaps that was true in the beginning, another part of her cried silently. Perhaps it was still true. But she couldn't blame him for whatever he felt. If she didn't— perhaps in time it would be her that he really wanted instead of Marnie. Leslie knew that she was rationalizing, but she couldn't stop herself. She loved him, and she wanted him so desperately that she no longer had the self-control to follow the dictates of her rational mind.

They danced again and again. Their bodies flowed so

smoothly together it seemed they were made for each other. The hours of the evening wore quickly away, and it was late when Boone suggested that they leave.

This time when Boone turned off the highway Leslie recognized the road that twisted up the mountain drive to Boone's house.

"Boone, I really think that you should take me home," she forced herself to insist.

"That's exactly what I'm doing," he said, deliberately misunderstanding her. The sensual line of his mouth quirked in tender amusement, as his hand moved to caress her shoulder.

"That's not what I meant," she whispered.

"I know. But it's what you want," came his husky reply. "Admit it."

It was all too true. "I don't seem to be able to be smart where you're concerned," she said softly. "I went to bed with you the first night I met you. I should have learned my lesson."

"I'm tired of smart women," he said quietly, his low voice strangely cool as he removed his hands from her shoulders.

She'd said something wrong, but she didn't know what. Had she somehow reminded him of Marnie? At the mere thought of his wife her chest ached as though a tight band had been drawn around it.

"You know I'm right," she insisted, testing. "I'm not just talking about us. If a woman goes to bed with a man right off, he can't ever really care for her. She should wait . . ."

"Until she's got her hooks so deeply into him, he can't get away," Boone muttered savagely more to himself than to her. Then he drew a deep breath as though to control his anger.

Dimly she was aware of Boone flicking the button on his visor and of the garage door opening. Abruptly Boone braked the car and pressed the button once more. The door shut silently, and Boone switched off the ignition. They were wrapped in total darkness. She shifted uneasily, but he caught her against his hard strength.

"I'm too old for all those games, Leslie. Maybe they make sense for teenagers. I hope so, because all those rules drive you crazy as hell when you're young. All I know is I want you more than I've ever wanted any woman. Why should I do without you when I know you feel the same way?"

He'd said he wanted her more than he'd ever wanted any woman. For a brief moment happiness filled her. Did he include Marnie? And then her joy faded as doubt reasserted itself. Or was it just that he thought of her as Marnie—in a physical sense?

"Things aren't that simple, Boone," she said gently.

"They are if you'll let them be."

"But, I can't . . ."

"Sure you can. I'm going to show you how . . . tonight. . . ."

"Boone . . ." she protested weakly.

She felt the imprint of his finger against her lips, gently shushing her.

"You talk too much. You know that don't you?" he whispered into the soft swirling darkness as he pulled her into his arms.

She was about to answer his question when his mouth

closed over hers, forcing back her reply as he explored the velvety softness of her lips. She felt limp as a strange yielding weakness enveloped her and yet more alive than she'd ever felt before. Every sense seemed more acute.

She felt the roughness of his cheek graze her own, satiny smooth face. He tasted deliciously of brandy. She caught the scent of him—his heady, clean, male fragrance mingling with his aftershave. After a long kiss that made her reel in a world that contained nothing except whirling darkness and her fevered awareness of him, he drew his lips away. He inhaled a deep, long breath.

She was so hot, she felt she glowed. Her voluptuous curves trembled against the lean, hard contours of his body.

"Kiss me again," she begged softly.

Lightly his lips gave her nose a chaste peck, and she emitted a tiny, disappointed sigh.

"Not like that," she murmured huskily.

"If we're going to stop," he said, "it'd better be now. Do you still want me to drive you home?"

Slowly, all evening he'd sought to awaken her to the sensual needs she fought to conquer. Desire burned through her as hot as a raging conflagration.

"Love me. . . ." she surrendered weakly.

8

~~~~~~~~~~

Love me. . . ." Leslie's softly spoken words lingered in the black silence.

"I thought you'd never ask," Boone murmured silkily, gathering her warm body into his arms.

Dreamily she let him lead her inside up a circular staircase to a vast, utterly masculine bedroom. She scarcely noticed the brass kingsize bed, the tans and golds, the leather furniture. A great brown bear rug stretched across the dark wood floor, and she saw it just as he pulled her down onto the thick fur.

He lay sprawled across the fur beneath her while she sat beside him, her hips lightly touching his waist. From beneath the hooded sweep of thick lashes she stared deeply into the shimmering darkness of his eyes.

He reached up and traced a finger from her chin over her soft throat to the edge of her red silk dress. Long brown fingers played with the tiny silken bow at her neckline, loosening it so that her dress fell open, exposing creamy breasts encased in delicate white lace. He tugged at the string once more, and the edge of her dress fell a tantalizing inch further, baring her shoulder. He ran a roughened fingertip across the shadowed hollow between the fullness of her breasts. At his touch she sighed, shivering. She was drowning in a sea of exquisite sensations. As he pulled her down against him, she abandoned herself to the extravagant, languorous sexual pleasure only he could give her.

Slowly their clothes were removed, and as she lay on top of him his eyes skimmed her satiny body downward over her breasts that gently rose and fell with each breath, the flat smoothness of her belly, down to her well-turned hips. He thought her inutterably lovely. Her yellow hair, casually disheveled from his loveplay, gleamed like liquid gold in the pale light.

She stared down at him lovingly. He lay sprawled with indolent grace across the rug. Her arms wrapped around him, and he pulled her down against his great hard-muscled chest and hungrily plundered her lips. Then he caressed her body with his warm hands, trailing his fingers down the curve of her spine and over her hips. Lightly he explored her thighs and the sensitive flesh between her legs.

His intimate touch, his wild kisses, his possessive words of endearment muttered hoarsely against her ear drew her deeper and deeper into a hot, wondrous world of desire. Her emerald eyes glowed with fire; her skin burned with feverish need.

When he pulled her even closer and pressed his hard lean body against the yielding softness of her own, she cried out, a gentle, muted cry of ecstasy. A faint tremor of emotion rippled through her like a tiny wave. This new feeling grew, surging through her, until she surrendered herself to him completely, clinging to him with a desperate need.

The fierce blaze of their love was like a splendid, soaring flame against an ink-black sky—brilliant and beautiful, primitive and wild.

After that they lay together for a long time, shuddering, and then they were still. A warm brown hand gently stroked through the golden disorder of her hair. He stared deeply into her eyes, and in that moment she believed that she meant more to him than he could say.

He made love to her again and again that night, wanting her to need him as he needed her, wanting her to cry out for him, demanding that she do so. Leslie gave herself to him with a total completeness that was even greater than the first night he'd possessed her. She loved him hopelessly, shamelessly, as he awakened her body again and again to new and wanton pleasures.

At last they fell asleep wrapped in one another's arms, the warmth of his breath against the softness of her breast, the gentle beat of her heart beneath his ear.

Outside it was gray dark when Boone's lips nuzzling against Leslie's throat awakened her.

A faint golden glow tinged the mountain top, hinting that it would soon be daylight.

Gently Boone's hand roamed over her belly. Drowsy yet from the long night of love, her emerald eyes opened slowly and lifted to his. She smiled a slow sweet smile, the smile of a woman sated from her lover's caresses, and he returned her smile with a tender one of his own.

The passionate tenderness of his gaze warmed her

through. All the months of loneliness were washed away, and she felt that she had at last found a man with whom she could share her life, to whom she could give her heart and her soul. Without love, life had seemed unbearably empty. She hadn't realized until this moment of sharing, just how empty.

"Lazy bones," he gently teased. "We're going to have to get up if we're to get to work on time."

"Slave driver," she accused lightly, sitting up. The sheet fell away, exposing the voluptuous curve of creamy breasts for his keen, masculine appraisal.

His lips descended to kiss a nipple. Then he rose and strode before it was too late across the room to the bathroom. She heard his deep voice as he sang in the shower, and impulsively she scampered lightly across the cool oak floor and flung open the shower door.

"Mind if I join you?" Her impish smile illuminated her delicate features.

Dark, gleaming eyes roved over her. In answer, a bronzed arm wrapped around her narrow waist and pulled her inside. His hard male body crushed her against the steaming tiles as the warm spray of water flowed over them.

"Boone, my hair . . ." she protested softly.

His body moved against her, communicating his rising need.

"You should have thought about that before you came in here," he muttered fiercely. "To hell with your hair. . . ."

Thus began the first day of a week of such glorious days and nights. Every free moment that they could steal away from the pressures of work, they spent together, reveling in the exquisite sensual pleasure each could give the other. Though Boone never told her he loved her, he showed her in a hundred small ways that he cared.

Twice when he had to drive into Denver he arranged for her to go with him, as though he couldn't bear to be parted from her any longer than he had to be. When he couldn't take her with him, he called frequently.

Every afternoon they lunched together at some new and charmingly different restaurant. He took her ski touring all over Snowpeak, explaining all his plans for its development, sharing his dreams. Every day she sensed his trust in her growing a little more. But still he never told her about Marnie. Nor did he make any explanations for his bitterness toward women. Leslie knew he was still bitter, even though he tried very hard to conceal this from her.

She thought he was trying to find happiness in their present, that he deliberately sought to disregard their future because he was too cynical to believe that what they had together could last. For the time being, Leslie was content to do as he did.

Some part of Leslie warned her that she was foolish to take so much joy in the present without considering the future, without forcing a commitment. But she couldn't stop herself. She was committed irrevocably. She loved Boone and needed him too much to deny him anything. If he needed time, she would give him time. Whenever they were together her doubts would drain away, and she would wonder how anything could go wrong when they were so blissfully happy.

This euphoric state was abruptly shattered late one afternoon. Leslie was fumbling in her handbag for her keys outside her front door when the telephone inside her condominium began to ring. Thinking it might be Boone, she made a special effort to catch it. In the middle of the fifth ring, she breathlessly lifted it to her ear.

"Hello," she gasped.

"Hi, Les, it's me," came the all-too-familiar, Texas drawl of her "ex."

"Tim. . . ." A chill swept through Leslie, and she clutched the receiver more tightly. She'd been so wrapped up in Boone she'd scarcely given Karen or her imminent return a thought.

"From that husky voice of yours it sounds like you were expecting someone else—someone more exciting," he jeered lightly.

A wave of irritation washed through her. He knew her too well.

"That's certainly none of your business anymore!" she snapped.

Ignoring her burst of temper his bland drawl continued. "I was just giving you a call to let you know about my plans for tomorrow, the thirty-first."

She'd completely forgotten about her date with Tim for New Year's Eve. Her throat was suddenly dry at the thought of having to explain this ticklish situation to Boone.

Tim's voice continued, and she had to force herself to concentrate on what he was saying. "Karen and I'll get to Denver around twelve. I have to rent a car. I guess that'll put us in Winter Park around three in the afternoon."

Fear rippled through her at the thought of telling Boone. What was she going to do? Instantly she knew she had no choice but to talk Tim out of going out with her.

"Tim, I–I can't go out with you. . . . I'm dating someone else . . . someone special. . . ."

"So am I."

"But he won't like . . . me going out with you."

"Look, you and I made a date two weeks ago, and if you're set on breaking it at the last minute you can tell Karen yourself." There was a hard edge to his voice. "I'm going to put Karen on the phone right now."

"Tim . . ."

"Hi, Mommy."

"Karen, darling. . . . I was just trying to tell your daddy that it's really silly for he and I to go out now that we're divorced."

The long hushed silence grew increasingly awkward between them.

"Karen, are you there?" Desperately, she pressed on. "Karen?" A bitter sob was clearly audible on the other end of the line, but the child made no other response. "Karen?"

"You promised," Karen finally choked. "You promised you'd be nice to Daddy. If you break your promise, I'll never believe anything you say again!"

With that the line went dead.

For a long moment Leslie sat in numbed silence. She couldn't go back on her word to Karen. That was very clear to her. She would have to find a way to make Boone understand.

Tomorrow night she had a date with her exhusband! This unpleasant thought throbbed through her mind over and over again. How could she have forgotten that this was coming up? It was just that she'd been so absorbed in Boone that all the realities had blurred. All week when she'd forgotten appointments or slept through her alarm, she'd laughed indulgently at herself, knowing the reason for her absent-mindedness. But now she couldn't laugh.

She'd completely forgotten about New Year's Eve. Boone had never mentioned the evening, and she just hadn't thought. . . .

She would have to tell him at once, even though she instinctively knew he wasn't going to like it. He was so fiercely possessive.

Glancing down at her delicate gold wristwatch, she realized she would be seeing him soon since he was planning to bring steaks over and cook them at her place at seven. Before Tim's call, she'd looked forward to the evening. But now a vague apprehension coursed through her as she tried to think of a way to tell him about Tim. The afternoon passed all too quickly.

That night when she opened her door to greet Boone, tension trembled through her as his possessive gaze roamed over her, lingering where her bare nipples pushed against sheer, cream silk. A bright flush tinged her cheeks as she remembered she was braless. She'd omitted the lacy undergarment at his own request. What had he whispered this morning in the privacy of his office? "Don't wear anything under your clothes tonight. We're not going out. It'll make it less trouble to undress you. . . ."

He was looking at her warmly, as though she were his alone. How was she going to tell him she planned to spend the next evening with another man? The mere thought made her flinch.

As always the sheer male size of him overwhelmed her, and she gasped. He was breathtakingly handsome. A pale blue western shirt was stretched tautly across his massive chest; faded jeans molded his lean hips. Slung over one shoulder was his familiar sheepskin coat.

He extended a brown grocery sack which contained two steaks, and she took it, leaving him briefly at the door while she took them to the refrigerator. He was still lounging indolently against the door frame when she returned. She realized with a blush that he'd been watching her intently. His eyes traveled upward from the gentle swaying movements of her hips to the faint bouncing of her full breasts beneath sheer silk. His avid stare was all male. A tiny thrill that she, by simply walking across a room, could arouse him, overcame her.

Golden light glinted in his jet-dark hair as he stepped lithely inside. His black eyes roved over her, the heat of his gaze stripping away her clothes as his hands had so often done recently. She flushed again prettily. She noticed for the first time that his tanned features were more harshly drawn than of late, and she remembered he'd had an important meeting with the County Planning Commission about Snowpeak this afternoon. In spite of her anxiety, the mere sight of him stirred her pulse, and she slipped her hand into his.

"How did things go this afternoon?" she asked as he led her toward the bar.

"Bad." He ground out the word as he remembered. "I've got a real fight on my hands with the County Planning Commission over zoning."

"Oh . . ." She watched worriedly as he poured himself a double Scotch on the rocks and then mixed a shot of Scotch with water for her.

"I'll probably have to waste valuable time fighting, but I'm sure I'll get what I want in the end. I've been through this sort of thing before." He smiled grimly down at her, and her exquisite loveliness caused his expression to soften. "But I didn't come over here to worry about all that. What I want to do is relax—with you. I've had enough problems thrown at me for one day."

There was a fierce, dark element in his voice that struck a note of foreboding in her heart, increasing her anxiety as she remembered she had planned to tell him about Tim tonight.

Drawing her down onto the couch beside him, he set his drink on the end table. His black eyes slid over her. Then his lips quirked in a slanting smile that disturbed her emotional equilibrium.

"I know something that'll do me a lot more good than that drink," he murmured, gazing deeply into her eyes.

"What?"

"You." His low tone vibrated through her, tingling every nerve end in her body.

Before she could reply he lowered his dark face toward hers, and she felt the bruising pressure of his mouth, forcing her lips open so that his hot moist tongue could enter and probe. Moving one of his hands through her golden curls, he tilted her head backward so that he could more intimately explore the soft voluptuous curve of her lips. His other hand unbuttoned the tiny fastenings of her silk blouse, and as the blouse slid down her creamy shoulders, his hand moved over her bare breasts, cupping them before his mouth descended to ravish their love-swollen tips.

"Leslie, you drive me wild," he muttered thickly, his warm breath tickling the bare flesh beneath her breast. "I can't wait. . . . tonight . . . I have to have you . . . now. . . ."

The raw urgency in his deep voice shivered through

her. Even though she sensed that her body was like the double Scotch he'd poured himself—a means of forgetting his problems—she ached for him.

His lips sent searing waves trembling through her nervous system until she was as wildly delirious for him as he was for her. As he nuzzled her, caressing the ripe fullness of her breast with his large hands, nibbling at a nipple with his mouth, a slow, erotic fire began to burn in the depths of her being. She moaned softly, arching her body so that his raven head was buried in the opulent lushness of her breasts, so that he could continue to explore their soft fullness.

He shifted his body. The hard muscular strength of his arms imprisoned her against the massive wall of his chest. She was very aware of the blistering heat of his skin burning her through the coarse fabric of his western shirt. She felt the hard imprint of his male desire against her lower body.

The compelling force of his passion shuddered through him, as he held her tightly against him. She felt the wild pace of his heart; she heard the ragged intake of his breaths.

Leslie could do nothing but surrender to the powerful force of his desire. He needed her. He ached for her, and she reveled, she gloried in her feminine power over this virile man.

Need as fierce as his own drove her as her shaking fingers unsnapped his shirt, ripping it apart so that a strip of lean brown flesh was exposed. For a while her lips roamed over him. Then her slender hands explored lower, undressing him completely.

She wanted him to know how much she loved him, how completely she was his, how completely she wanted him to be hers. And there seemed to be only one way of showing him.

Slowly, in a mindless love trance, she lowered her lips to his skin and kissed the hard, warm flesh—tentatively at first and then more confidently, reveling in his complete and total masculinity, wanting to know him more intimately than she'd ever known any man. She caught the faint tang of his male scent and was inflamed by the intensity of his response to her.

He groaned beneath the steady onslaught of her exploring mouth. "Leslie . . ." he rasped her name. She felt his hands, heavy in the cascading masses of her golden hair as she made love to him in a way that she'd never done before. She told him with the exquisite wet softness of her lips what she couldn't yet tell him with words—that for her there would never be another man but him.

All that she did roused her own desire, but her need was not as important to her as his. And when he lost himself completely in wave upon wave of sensation, she at last lay upon him for a long time, savoring the wonder of her rapturous feelings for him. She felt the heat of his languid gaze scanning her face as though to memorize the loveliness of her features, and at the memory of what she had just done, she flushed bright crimson.

"Leslie . . ." His deep voice was hoarse from emotion; the mere sound of it was a sensual caress.

Then his mouth lowered to hers, crushing her unsuspecting lips in a kiss that obliterated all shame, everything save the hard feel of his mouth plundering hers. The force of his kiss wiped away all, leaving only an aching awareness of him. Liquid fire raced through her arteries as he ignited a passion that only he could quench.

He released her mouth only to pick her up in his arms, cradling her soft voluptuous curves against his hard, masculine body. Then with long strides, he carried her toward her bedroom.

"Boone, what are you doing?" she murmured weakly.

"I want to give you as much pleasure as you just gave me," he said gently into her flowing hair, as he lay her down between crisp, laundry-fresh sheets upon the vast softness of her bed.

Shyly, "You don't have to . . ."

Her words trailed away into a haze of sexual oblivion as his mouth sought her source of passion, and a tiny quiver of pulsating wildness shivered through her. She knew no shame at the intimacy of his embrace. She had no thought of resisting him, no will to do so. Instead she melted against the heat of his expert lips and hands that knew where and how to touch a woman to produce the most exquisite sensations until she was aching with delightful torment. As his mouth brought her to new peaks of shuddering ecstasy, she cried out his name again and again, clutching him to her as she savored the wanton splendor of passionate release.

Making love to her thus had aroused his own fierce ardor once more. After allowing her a brief rest he made love to her again—his touch, his lips stirring her once more so that she was consumed with the wildly pagan need for his love. Their fierce lovemaking bound them together in love's wanton dance for a timeless time. When it was over she lay on top of him, using his great warm body as a bed, the vast expanse of his chest as her pillow. His arms were draped over her in careless, familiar possession.

Much later, as they lay satiated in one another's arms,

she stirred drowsily and nipped the bottom edge of his ear before murmuring into it. "You've been here for hours, and we still haven't eaten those steaks."

"Somehow I haven't given that a thought." His lips quirked in dry amusement.

"We're going to have to get up before too long and cook."

"I'm not sure I have the strength," he teased gently, drawing her closer.

"I'm not sure I do either," she whispered, nibbling at his earlobe again.

"And I don't have the strength for that either," he smiled.

But she did not heed him. Instead her lips continued their seductive exploration, and in a very short time she proved him wrong.

"Vixen . . ." The word was a husky endearment, lingering on his lips as his black gaze caressed her. "You're the only good thing that happened today."

"Thank you," she returned softly.

"You never did tell me about your afternoon," he murmured. "Was it as bad as mine?"

The unexpected question caused her to remember what had happened, and the memory of Tim's phone call jolted through her. She blanched slightly.

"Something wrong?" he asked, noting that she'd suddenly gone pale.

The drowsy passionate languor in his eyes matched her own feelings of a moment before. If she told him about Tim now, the mood would be radically changed.

Still now was the time to tell him about Tim, she told

herself wildly. But as she stared into his deep dark eyes, the words wouldn't come. She rationalized her desire to procrastinate by telling herself he'd had such a hard day she couldn't burden him with this . . . just yet. Not now, when he'd finally managed to put the cares of the day behind him. Besides she knew telling him would spoil the marvelous spell their lovemaking had cast over them. And she couldn't bear to do that.

But as she gazed into the blackened depths of his eyes, she quivered. She saw the unrelenting hardness and strength in his implacable features, and she remembered when he'd been cold and hard to her. She couldn't bear it if he turned against her again. What if he did that when she told him?

How was she ever going to summon the courage to tell him? When? A tiny pulsebeat pounded in her head. She knew that it had to be soon.

After dinner . . . she promised herself desperately. She would tell him after dinner. She would procrastinate until after he'd eaten.

Boone lifted the last bite of steak to his lips, and Leslie watched with an utterly feminine satisfaction that this man had devoured with such relish the meal she had prepared for him.

When he finished eating he said, "I should have asked you about this sooner, but to tell you the truth I've been so preoccupied both with Snowpeak and with . . . you," his husky voice wrapped her with a sensual warmth that made her heart flutter happily, "that I completely forgot about New Year's Eve until Rose Mary reminded me that Yvonne, my cousin, was coming down and that we all ought to go somewhere. Anyway, this afternoon I bought tickets for the dance at the Devil's Brand Ranch."

This announcement was as unexpected as it was upsetting. A tiny quiver of dread began to pound in Leslie's throat. Suddenly her throat felt dry and parched as though she were dying of thirst in a desert. Inadvertently she lifted her wineglass and drained it.

"Is something wrong, Leslie? You're as white as a sheet!" His black, intent gaze bored through her.

"Boone . . . I . . ."

"What is it?"

"Karen's coming home tomorrow. I . . ."

"I'd forgotten about that. But, if you'd like, we could include her in our plans. The dance is a family affair and they have activities for children; however, if you'd prefer for the three of us to spend a quiet evening together, I can return the tickets. Mother would understand."

"Boone, I can't go out with you." Her tongue felt like a huge dry thing that she could scarcely move between her lips.

A new hardness shone in his dark gaze that terrified her. But when he spoke, his voice betrayed no emotion. "Why not?" he asked.

"B–because Tim's coming too," she said softly.

"What does that have to do with us?" There was a vague coldness in his deep tone that chilled her.

"N–nothing . . . except . . ." She broke off. Why was he making this so difficult?

"Except what?" he demanded.

"I made a foolish promise . . ."

"Go on . . ."

She could no longer meet his level gaze.

"To go out with him."

His expression darkened, the sudden blazing passion in his eyes searing her heart with an odd pain. Vaguely she was aware of the fierce pressure of his fingers gripping her shoulders. She felt herself floundering helplessly like a swimmer washed overboard in the furious storm of his wrath.

"What?" His single word thundered through her.

"I'm going out with Tim tomorrow night," she said desperately. The dark shuttered look that she remembered so well and hated masked all of his emotion. "I don't want to. I don't! Oh, please! Boone! Don't look at me like that! Don't shut me out!"

But even as she begged him to believe her, he shrugged her from him and strode toward the glass door that opened onto her balcony. He stared broodingly out onto the glistening snowy landscape.

Quickly she followed him, but when she reached out to him, he said curtly, "Stay away from me . . . Leslie. The last thing I want right now is for you to touch me."

She heard the coldness in his voice that told her more clearly than anything he could have said that he didn't believe her, that he couldn't trust her, that he again saw her as the kind of woman he hated. And something very precious deep in her heart shattered.

"What was I?" he asked at last, his wintry eyes piercing her soul, "A passionate diversion, while you waited for him. . . . A delightful interlude to keep your boredom at bay. . . ." His deep self-mockery coiled around her, strangling her emotionally.

"No . . . Boone, you know that's not the way it is between us."

131

"No, Leslie, I don't," he said very quietly. "I thought I knew you. But now I see that I don't know you at all. And I'm not even sure I want to."

At the cold finality in his tone, she shivered. As she stared past him out the window, her heart seemed as bleak and empty as the snowy vastness of the valley outside.

9

"Please, Boone, try to understand," she pleaded.

"I am trying, Leslie. But it's damned difficult when I think of you planning to go out with the man you were once married to."

"It doesn't mean anything, Boone."

"Maybe not to you. But what about him? And me? Have you given it any thought what it does to a man when a woman strings him along?"

"I'm not stringing either of you along. I told him how I feel, and I've told you the truth about tomorrow night."

The blistering heat of his gaze told her that he wanted to believe her, but some demon from his past prevented it. He couldn't trust her.

"Where are you two going . . . tomorrow night?" he asked in an even, dead tone, as though he no longer really cared.

"I have a date with him to the Devil's Brand Ranch."

"That figures!"

"Oh, Boone, I don't want to go out with him. I really don't! I told him I would two weeks ago . . . before . . . us. . . ."

"Then break your date!" he snapped.

"I tried to this afternoon. But I couldn't."

"You could if you wanted to."

"It's not that simple."

"Of course it is. Leslie, there's no point in arguing over this. I have a long day tomorrow."

"Will you please listen to me while I try to explain."

"That's what I thought I've been doing. You were telling me that you couldn't break your date."

"It's because of Karen," she said weakly.

"What in the hell does Karen have to do with any of this?"

"I'm going out with Tim because of her."

"Leslie, I don't believe that for one minute. You're an adult. Don't blame your desire to go out with Tim on your child."

"It's the truth."

"Just what in the hell kind of woman are you anyway?" he rasped. Suddenly his arms were around her like hard, tight bands, imprisoning her against him. His black eyes glittered as they swept over her, devouring her fragile loveliness. "When you made love to me a while ago I thought you gave yourself to me completely, and all the time you were planning . . . this. It's obvious you don't give a damn about either of us. But I suppose that dangling two men from some emotional string satisfies some basic need in your ego. The thing that really gets me is that for the life of me, I don't understand myself.

How could I have been so taken in . . . the second time around."

Abruptly he released her and strode briskly across the living room. He was lifting his sheepskin coat from the armchair by the door and swinging it across his broad shoulder. He was leaving her, and she knew that this time he wouldn't be coming back.

"Boone, don't go. Please . . ."

Quickly she followed him to the door. Her slender hand reached out and gripped his arm. The minute she touched him, he recoiled as though burned. Then he swept her once more into his arms, and stared savagely down at her, with a look of utter disgust stamped into his hard, angry profile.

"How can anyone as beautiful as you are be the way you are?" he demanded roughly.

"I'm not like what you think, Boone," she pleaded desperately. "I'm not . . ."

He felt his anger melting. Her frantic sincerity almost penetrated the shell of his defenses. Her eyes were overly large like great shimmering liquid emeralds. Tears spilled over her long lashes and down the creamy softness of her cheeks.

At the sight of her so desperately vulnerable, he stiffened, rejecting the impulse to relent. She looked exactly like a wounded animal, and the powerful urge to cradle her against him and protect her rose up in him.

But he forced himself to loosen his grip on her slender shoulders and set her from him. He shot her a cold, hard look of farewell. As she gazed for the last time on his beloved, chiseled features, little did she know how close he'd come to giving in to the message of his heart.

* * *

When Boone had gone, Leslie lay on the couch in a daze. Tears streamed over her face, but she was scarcely aware that they did. Her whole body shook as she remembered his savage rejection.

He'd left her, and he wasn't coming back! This thought made her heart pound like a heavy gong of doom. How could she have known two weeks ago when she'd told Tim she'd go out with him that things could have changed between herself and Boone? And now after nearly two weeks of utter happiness, losing him was like death itself.

What was she going to do? She couldn't bear to lose him. And all because of a stupid, idiotic misunderstanding that was somehow tied to his past distrust of women. Something had happened to him that had scarred him so deeply, that he wouldn't even try to believe her. Instead he was associating her with the woman in his past who'd hurt him.

It wasn't fair! her heart protested. She could scarcely breathe. The bitter pain in her chest was suffocating her. And yet as the night wore into the early hours of the morning, the intensity of her pain lessened until she felt nothing except a curious numbness.

The next morning black shadows were etched like tiny black moons beneath her eyes; her complexion was utterly colorless. Because of the holiday, she didn't have to work. Otherwise she would have had to call in sick. She simply couldn't face anyone—not yet when she was totally devastated emotionally.

After she'd cleaned up the apartment and washed and rolled her hair, she sank onto her bed in a state of sheer exhaustion and fell sound asleep only to awaken later to the insistent ring of the telephone on her bedside table.

Hope that it was Boone made her heart flutter madly, and then at the sound of Tim's flat drawl, it seemed to stop completely.

She drew a slow agonized breath.

"Les, Karen and I are running a little late. Our plane just got to Denver. We won't get up to Winter Park until around five."

"I'll be here," she replied dully before they hung up.

An hour before Tim was to arrive she rose listlessly and began to dress for the evening. A white stick of makeup erased the remnants of the shadows beneath her eyes. Her perfumed hair tumbled over her shoulders, glistening. As she expertly made up her face, she never gave Tim or how he might react to her now that she dressed so glamorously a thought. Once she would have given anything for an evening with him, to prove that she was the attractive woman he'd said she could never be.

But now . . . tonight . . . nothing mattered except Boone.

Leslie had time to read the Winter Park newspaper. She was shocked to read that a skier who'd missed the last bus to town had tried hitchhiking and had been picked up by two men who raped her.

Crime was supposed to be nonexistent in Winter Park! As the doorbell buzzed Leslie refolded the paper. She felt shaken. How many times had she driven out that way and shown property all by herself late in the afternoon without ever giving her personal safety a thought?

As Leslie opened the door Karen dashed into the

livingroom and into her mother's arms, heedlessly crushing the low-cut rose silk gown that Leslie was wearing. Karen's exuberant greeting washed a little of Leslie's pain concerning Boone away, and as Leslie lifted her lovely eyes to Tim's, her smile was artlessly radiant.

Blue eyes gleamed with a strange light as Tim stared uncomprehendingly down at the exquisite woman he'd so rashly divorced. She had changed so that he hardly recognized her.

As Leslie stood up slowly, still clasping Karen's hand tightly in her own, she thought Tim no different than he'd ever been. The only difference was her own reaction to his Nordic, blond handsomeness. Once she'd loved him, and now she was amazed that he inspired no more than a cool friendliness.

She was completely indifferent to him as a man. For the first time she was glad that he'd insisted on coming because she was at last free from him, from all the hurt he'd caused her when he'd walked out. If he hadn't come, she might never have known how completely she was over him.

Why was he looking at her like that, as if he were seeing her for the first time, when they'd been married for eight years? The bright light in his eyes made her feel slightly uncomfortable as she extended her hand to welcome him into her home.

After the amenities had been exchanged, she was the first to draw her hand away from the clinging warmth of his grasp.

"Do we have time for a guided tour of Winter Park?" Tim asked lightly. "Before it gets dark."

"Yes, of course," Leslie replied mechanically. "And while we're out we can check you into a motel room."

"I thought Daddy would be staying here," Karen inserted.

"I made a reservation at a motel just down the way, Karen dear," Leslie replied firmly.

"But Mom . . ."

"Karen, your father and I are divorced. We have been for a very long time, and I think it's time you accepted it. I promised you I'd go out with him tonight, but that's as far as it goes."

Karen's dark brows creased together in a petulant frown, and she fought against the brimming tears as she headed sulkily toward her room.

"Leslie, was that really necessary?" Tim chided, a husky note that made her feel uneasy creeping into his voice. "I feel damned awkward not staying with my daughter and wife."

"I'm sorry for that, Tim," she returned sincerely, lifting her lovely emerald eyes to his. "But one thing you made very clear eighteen months ago was that you no longer wanted me for your wife."

His blue gaze slid over her. "Somehow seeing you . . . now . . . I still think of you as my wife."

"I'm sorry for you then," she returned quietly. "Because I no longer think of you as my husband."

Karen went next door to see Gini and her children, and Leslie suspected that this was a ruse to allow her parents some time alone together. Leslie used that time to drive Tim around Winter Park. She pointed out Karen's school, the ski slopes, and other points of local interest. Last of all they stopped at his motel, which happened to be directly across the highway from one of Boone's construction sites. Though he'd stopped building condominiums because of the weather, Boone frequently stopped by to check on them. She breathed a sigh of relief when she saw that the site was abandoned.

When she would have waited outside while Tim went into the motel, he insisted she come inside.

"You're being ridiculous, you know," Tim admonished with mock severity. "You could freeze to death out here while I take a shower."

"I suppose you're right," she said at last, remembering that Tim took notoriously long showers.

"Besides you should know me well enough to know I've never yet taken advantage of an unwilling woman."

His smile was infectious, and to her surprise she found herself returning it. The thought of cool, debonair Tim resorting to violence of any kind struck her as humorous.

An hour later Tim and she emerged from his motel suite. She'd read several articles in a news magazine he'd given her while he had unpacked and showered.

As Tim helped her into the passenger side of her car and slipped behind the wheel himself, she noticed Boone's truck parked on the opposite side of the highway. Just as Tim pulled out onto the highway, Boone strode from around the back of the project out into the golden sunlight.

His black hair was ruffled and tossed with golden highlights. His tanned features were harshly set. Never had she been so aware of anyone as she was of him in that moment. For a moment the dark outline of his hard male form blurred, and she fought back the burning tears that just the sight of him produced.

Then she felt his black, searing gaze touch her, before he quickly looked away as though she were the last person on earth he wanted to see or think of. Never had she felt so totally rejected.

As Tim sped toward her condominium over snow-packed roads, fleetingly she wondered how long Boone had been there. Had he seen her car at the motel? Had he only stopped to see how long she stayed at Tim's motel room? Did he think that she and Tim . . .

Suddenly she sensed with absolute certainty that Boone thought her fully capable of sleeping with Tim even though yesterday she'd tried to show him the depth of her feelings for him. Couldn't he understand that for her he was the only man in all the world? That not even Tim had ever meant to her what he did?

It was all too obvious the answer was no.

Karen had gone to spend the night with Gini and her children. Again, though Karen's manipulations made Leslie feel uncomfortable, Leslie could only admire her child's determination to provide the proper setting for her parents' reunion.

"And so," Tim was saying as he maneuvered her car down the road toward Devil's Brand Ranch, his smooth drawl self-deprecatory, "we have the whole night . . . together."

"Not quite," Leslie responded dryly.

"That's only because you insist," he persisted, braking the car in front of the sprawling dude ranch house.

"Tim, I wish you would quit . . . teasing me."

"Leslie, I think you know me well enough to know I'm not teasing."

Leslie sighed heavily and burrowed more deeply into her silver fur as he got out and walked briskly around the front of the car to her door.

It was going to be a very long evening if Tim kept this up, and in her battered emotional state she wasn't sure she was up to coping with him.

Apparently the Devil's Brand Ranch party was the most widely attended New Year's Eve party within a sixty-mile radius. Both locals and skiers packed the rambling ranch house. The band played a lively mixture of country-western music and rock.

In spite of herself, Leslie found some of her tension abating as Tim and she chatted with the other guests. Now that she no longer desired Tim, now that all the old hurts he'd inflicted seemed to belong to the past, there was a new easiness growing between them, a brother-sister easiness that can only exist between a man and a woman who know each other very well.

As the evening wore on, Leslie found herself occasionally laughing. She danced often with the men who sat at their table, just as Tim danced often with the women.

They'd been at the party for nearly two hours and she and Tim were dancing together when Tim whispered into her ear, "Don't look now but that arrogant black-haired bastard who just walked in is staring holes through us."

A shiver of apprehension raced through Leslie, and missing a step, she clung more tightly to Tim for support.

She could not stop her gaze from slanting to the tall dark man who had just entered the room. Her misting eyes met the angry blackness of his for a long moment before she looked away. His gaze swept knowingly over her, stripping away her clothes in such a boldly insolent fashion that Leslie turned a deep shade of rose that matched her dress.

Grasping the sleeve of Boone's dinner jacket was a beautiful girl who was much younger than he. Glossy black ringlets framed the delicate oval of her face. She was petite and didn't even come up to his shoulder.

Tim winced, feeling the cutting edge of Leslie's long finger nails through the heavy fabric of his suit as, unconsciously, Leslie tightened her grip.

"So that's him," Tim stated baldly, with the maddening perception only an exhusband could have.

"Who?"

"The man you're dating . . . who you said was special."

"Y–yes. . . ."

"That girl he's with is . . . quite something."

"Y–yes. Isn't she?" Leslie's voice was strangely faint, and once again she missed a step.

"Who is she?" Tim persisted.

"I don't know. Maybe it's his cousin. He said something about an out-of-town cousin."

"For your sake I hope so," he mocked gently before he swept her down the length of the dance floor until they were out of range of Boone's vision.

Some time later Tim was pouring Leslie some punch.

"I'm sorry I came," he apologized, looking gently down at her with genuine affection.

"What do you mean?"

"Well, it's obvious you two are really in love. *He* can't take his eyes off you."

"He hates me now."

"I agree that he's very angry. Why didn't you explain that we planned this evening because of Karen."

"I tried to."

"But he's the possessive-macho type . . ."

"There's more to it than that, Tim, though I don't know exactly what."

"Well, since I've split you up, I'm going to do my best to help you get back together."

Some element in his voice startled her.

"Tim, what are you going to do?"

He nodded his blond head in the direction of the small, beautiful girl Boone had brought with him. Boone had left her by herself momentarily to get her a drink.

"I'm going to ask his date to dance. And that'll give you two a chance to make up."

"No, Tim, stay out of it," Leslie hissed. "He won't like it, and you'll just make matters worse!"

"Sorry, Les. I never was any good at taking orders . . . especially from you. Besides, this won't be a total act of charity. Other than you she's the best-looking woman at the dance. If she's really his cousin . . . Who knows? Maybe she goes for tall, dashing blonds. You know what they say—opposites attract."

"Tim!" she cried desperately after him, but he ignored her completely and moved with confident ease toward Boone's date.

"Just what in the hell does your husband think he's doing?" The hot anger in Boone's voice sliced through Leslie, and she whirled to face the tall, dark giant of a man who stood directly behind her.

Her luminous gaze met his fierce black one and held it. Tonight there was a bold recklessness about him, an element of sensual danger that heightened her feminine awareness of him, mesmerizing her.

"I don't really know," she replied uneasily.

"I believe you do," Boone insisted. "And I want an answer."

"I think he feels responsible for you being angry, and

he thought he'd help by asking your date to dance,"
Leslie replied tightly.

"The poor bastard. . . ." She caught the genuine pity
in his deep voice, as well as the condemning light in his
dark look. "He's so ensnared by you that he'll demean
himself by helping you make up with your lover."

Leslie tried to avert her gaze from the cold contempt in
his deep black eyes, but brown fingers moved quickly
and cupped her chin so that he could stare into her eyes.
She felt like an unjustly accused prisoner. Even so, his
mere touch sent a sensuous ripple tingling along her
nerve ends. Shivering she backed away, but he relent-
lessly pursued her until he'd cornered her against a wall.

"Or perhaps he's indifferent to me as a woman and
wants to help me . . . with you," Leslie reasoned. "He
and I have been divorced a year and a half. If he was so
wild about me, we wouldn't have separated."

"It never occurred to me that he had any choice in the
matter," Boone's deep, cold voice accused her.

"Then perhaps it should," she pleaded quietly. "He
left me because he wanted to date younger women. He
said I made him feel . . . old. . . ."

A black brow cocked in surprise. "I don't believe you,"
Boone said, very softly.

"What can I say then? I didn't believe it myself at first.
I'd never looked at any other man. I thought my
marriage would last forever, and then suddenly Tim
announces that he's bored."

"He what?"

"I know you think that only women can get tired of a
relationship and walk out. But men can do the same
thing. It happened to me."

"Somehow I don't think he's tired of you any more," Boone persisted. "I'll bet he'd take you back now . . . in a minute. I don't believe you make him feel old any longer."

Leslie paled momentarily at Boone's perception. At last she murmured, "If Tim's changed his mind, I can't be responsible for that. I couldn't have known. Boone . . . I only care about . . ."

The word "you" died in her throat at the brutal hardening of Boone's expression.

"And tell me . . ." he lashed out at her, "do you want your husband back? Or have you already taken him back . . . this afternoon in his motel room?"

Involuntarily Leslie's hand went to her throat and she drew a deep long breath. The atmosphere seemed suddenly dense and suffocating. A country-western tune whined loudly about a cheating woman and her hard-hearted lover. The pulsating beat of the song throbbed through Leslie. The acrid scent of cigarette smoke curled around her.

"Boone . . . I . . ." She broke off, so deeply hurt she was unable to deny what he accused her of. The harshness in his tone, the deep bitterness in his gaze betrayed how little he trusted her. Tears glazed her eyes, and she trembled.

"Did you?" His voice was low and deadly, and his hands closed over her wrist in a tight grip so that she couldn't escape.

Leslie's golden hair framed her pale features. Her green eyes were luminous as she stared desperately up at him.

Suddenly she saw that nothing she could say or do would make any difference to him. Boone had set his mind against her from the beginning. She remembered that first night when she'd made love to him and he'd turned against her, accusing her of being capable of only an empty, meaningless relationship. Suddenly she felt very tired. She saw the utter hopelessness of trying to make him believe in her.

"Boone, I don't have to tell you anything," she said weakly. "And I'm not going to. There's no use in my even trying to defend myself. I'm tired of trying to make you believe in me. Think the worst. And now . . . if you'll let go of me, I'd like to look for Tim. I'm tired, and I want to go home."

"Leslie . . ."

"There's nothing more I have to say to you, Boone. You and I are finished. I see that . . . now . . . as clearly as you do. I'm not going to try to explain myself to you any more. I've given up."

His dark face swam in her blurred vision for the briefest instant, and she blinked hard to hold back the tears.

"All right," he said at last. His roughly hewn profile appeared chiseled from granite. There was a new hardness about him, a roughness in his voice. "Have it your way. I think I knew all along you were no different than all the other women I've known . . ."

"No good," she finished for him, her voice quiet with defeat.

"You said it," he accused. "I didn't. But for the first time tonight we're in agreement. Go back to your husband . . . if he'll have you. I hold no claim on you."

Then he turned and stalked away. Out of her life, she knew, forever.

10

Tim left first thing the morning of the first, but not before he had a long talk with Karen. He tried to explain to their daughter that although Leslie and he were still her parents, they were divorced. There would never be a reconciliation. Karen listened to him and seemed to accept what he said.

Business was especially brisk at R.B. Dexter Inc. after the week-long holiday season. Leslie forced herself to work very hard, showing more property than normal in a vain attempt to keep from thinking about Boone.

A Mr. Ryan who owned Ryan Real Estate Company invited her to lunch on Friday. Leslie couldn't have been more surprised when he offered her a job.

"And so you see, Mrs. Grant," Mr. Ryan began, beaming at her from across the table after having explained his job offer, "we're willing to make it worth your while to move from Winter Park to Vail if you'll sell our property."

"You certainly are," she smiled, flipping through the sheaf of papers he'd handed her. "I'll have to go over these numbers and give your offer my careful consideration. Of course, I have a little girl, and I'd begun to think of Winter Park as home. I don't think she'll want to move."

"I think you'd like Vail." He flashed her a broad smile. "There's a lot more for a single person like yourself to do there. Why don't you come over this weekend and see the office? You could meet some of our personnel."

"I'd like that."

"Can you come Sunday?"

Thinking of Boone and the recent tension and hopelessness of their relationship, she replied, "All right."

Snow fell heavily all afternoon as it had for the past several days. Dynamite charges blasted through the mountains at regular half-hour intervals.

It was nearly four o'clock when Leslie returned from dropping Karen off at Gini's house to the office to pick up a set of keys to a custom-built house Boone had on the market. She was rustling through a drawer in Boone's office for the keys to the house when she heard his door open and close softly.

Leslie looked up straight into Boone's black eyes. His chiseled, rugged handsomeness affected her far more than she would have liked, and the bright glowing smile of welcome she tossed him was spontaneous. Why did she have to be so vulnerable to his masculine appeal? His black hair was mussed from the wind; tiny flecks of snow clung to its dark thickness. Her eyes drifted yearningly

149

over the wide stretch of his broad, muscular shoulders. He moved easily across the room toward her with the lithe grace that was a characteristic of his. Her smile faded almost at once at his own grim expression. The planes of his handsome face were set in harsh, implacable lines. The air in the room seemed suddenly to crackle with the rippling tension between them.

"I thought you were still in Denver," she said in a carefully light tone.

"Obviously." His one word was terse and sarcastic.

"What is that supposed to mean?" she asked quietly. "I was just looking for a key to the house at Hunter's Creek."

"What I meant was you would never have been in my office if you expected me," he explained. "You've been deliberately avoiding me all week."

"I thought that's what you wanted."

She felt the heat of his gaze flick indolently over the loveliness of her upturned face. For the briefest moment some emotion she didn't understand came and went in his dark eyes before he succeeded in repressing it. He tore his gaze from her beautiful face as though the mere sight of her affected him in a way he didn't like. "So it is," he returned coldly, leaning over his desk and picking up several files that had lain on top of it. His complete indifference to her caused an odd tight pain to compress her heart.

Leslie's fingers closed over the cool metal of the keys to the house, and she slipped the drawer shut. Straightening to her full height, she said coolly, "Then you'll be happy to learn that Sunday I'm driving over to Vail to look into the possibility of moving there."

For an instant his cool indifference was gone. "You're what?" His deep voice was hoarse.

"I received another job offer today that's so good I'm going to consider it."

What was she hoping for so desperately? That he'd say don't go, that he'd say their past differences didn't matter, that he'd say he understood why she'd had to go out with Tim? She should have realized the futility of such a hope.

"You and I have a contract." The menace in his cold tone wrapped around her as he moved nearer. No words of personal endearment, of wanting her for himself, softened his statement.

He towered over her; he was so close she caught the spiced tangy scent of his aftershave. She hated the quivering response of her traitorous body that made her intensely aware of him as a man, more so now that he was indifferent to her.

"I—I seem to remember you weren't too enthusiastic about signing it," she managed to say, forcing herself to meet his level gaze. "I'll need a job when that contract runs out, and it suddenly occurred to me that I would be foolish to wait until the last second to look for one, especially if one just falls into my lap."

"Your contract doesn't run out for nine more months. And when it does, I have every intention of offering you another one—with better terms."

Startled by his words, she lifted her gaze again to his. His face was a cool, dark mask, but she sensed a coiled tension about him. Did he dislike her so? Swallowing against the dryness in her throat, she suddenly realized she felt very nervous herself.

"I—I thought that under the circumstances . . . you'd prefer that I left," she said. "I made you sign that contract. You didn't want to. And now . . . this job offer could release us both from a difficult situation. Working with someone you've been personally involved with can pose problems . . . as you yourself once pointed out in the past."

"How eminently sensible you sound, Mrs. Grant," he taunted sarcastically. "What you say is . . . true. But as we're no longer personally involved, and we won't be in the future, I see no reason why we can't work together." He snapped the files he'd been holding shut and set them once more on his desk.

"Boone . . . I thought you'd be happy if I left."

His hard gaze raked over her softly vulnerable features, but if he liked what he saw he gave no indication of it. "Please don't confuse my motives for wanting to keep you on with my personal feelings for you," he said in a voice of steel. "My motives for wanting to keep you here are strictly related to business. You've proved you're damned good at selling real estate. I need good agents . . . whether or not I personally like them."

His compliment cut her more deeply than any insult, and she winced.

"Well, in that case," she began unsteadily, "I'd better get to work so that I can continue to deserve your approval. I'm supposed to show the Hunter's Creek house in fifteen minutes, and it's more than a ten-minute drive . . ."

"You're not planning to show that house tonight. . . ."

"I most certainly am," she returned defiantly.

"Where's your client?"

"He called me on the phone and said he'd meet me there at five."

"And you went along with that?" he demanded.

"Of course."

"I've told you in the past I don't want my women agents going out at night to meet clients they've never even seen."

"It's not night."

"It will be by the time you get out there. Besides, Hunter's Creek is very remote, and they've had some trouble out there. You know that's not far from where that girl got raped. There's several tumbling down rental houses that Carl Jacobs doesn't mind leasing to drifters. I don't want you up there on that lonely road in that little car of yours, especially when you're wearing next to nothing."

"Next to nothing . . ."

"That sweater clings to every curve—as you well know. If one of those men sees such a delectable piece of womanhood drive by on such a desolate stretch of road, who knows what he'll decide to do? I'm not sure you know how men think when they see a woman driving alone. It brings out their predatory instinct."

The unmistakable male interest in his black gaze that lingered insolently upon the swell of her breasts sent a swift hot current through her. Then his gaze slid boldly downward, stripping her. She felt embarrassed, and suddenly she was blushing furiously.

"I don't have to ask how you have come by your understanding of the masculine predatory instinct," she said with mock sweetness, wanting to insult him as his bold gaze insulted her.

His lips curved slightly with cynical humor. "Besides that danger, haven't you noticed that the weather's been steadily worsening all day? Look outside!" Glancing briefly out the window, she saw that snowflakes were blitzing downward in whirling fury. "You can hardly see through that stuff, much less drive in it. I'll bet you don't even have chains on your tires!"

"Yes, I do."

"Well, they're hardly fool-proof insurance in conditions like these. The snow control experts have been blasting to prevent avalanches all day! A woman shouldn't be out in such hazardous weather with or without chains. Call your client and cancel," he commanded. "That's an order."

"Boone . . ."

"You heard me. I don't want to be responsible for you up there at this hour."

Rage at what she considered an unreasonable, masculine, high-handed attitude surged through her as she marched briskly out of Boone's office and into her own. Quickly she searched through her appointment book for the telephone number of her client.

It wasn't that she wanted to drive up that mountain road alone; it was that she'd decided when Tim left her that if she were going to be a single woman on her own she couldn't let fear stop her from doing her job. She'd told herself she had to take care of herself like a man did. Just because she no longer had a husband to protect her didn't have to mean that she couldn't get out. She had a living to make for herself and her little girl. As a real estate agent she couldn't always show property during the day.

She rang the number twice, but there was no answer. Glancing at her watch, she realized she just had time to make the appointment if she disregarded Boone's order and left immediately.

Slipping behind the steering wheel of her car, she paused for a long moment to consider the wisdom of going against a direct command from Boone. It wasn't as if she were blatantly disregarding her boss's wishes. She'd tried to call her client and hadn't been able to reach him. Besides, she'd shown that house before, and nothing had happened. Boone was overreacting to the danger. Her client had the money to make this purchase if he decided to, and she hated the idea of standing him up. If she did that, it was highly likely he would find himself another agent and she would lose a sale.

Five minutes later all these well thought-out reasons for disobeying Boone seemed a little less sensible as the sun, concealed by the thickly falling snow, sank behind the mountains. The long, sweeping shadows made the forest on either side of the twisting mountain road eerie and gray. Since she'd left the outskirts of Winter Park, she hadn't passed a single car.

The snowbanks along the narrow, winding road were only knee-deep at first, but as she inched onward they gradually grew higher.

Slowly she drove past the row of shabby, tar-paper houses Boone had warned her of. A rusted pickup partially covered with a blanket of snow was parked in the road, but no one was in sight. She breathed a deep breath of relief.

The road twisted, and she could no longer see the houses in her rear-view mirror. She was nearly to her destination at Hunter's Creek when the snow began shooting down like white bullets, almost obliterating the road. For the first time she noticed that the snowbanks beside the road were deeper than the car was high. A newly posted sign almost buried in snow read "Hunter's Slide Area—No stopping or standing." In the silence she was aware of her pounding heartbeats. Never had she felt so alone.

The road was slick with ice and fresh snow. The snowbanks beside the road were so high now, she almost felt that she was driving through a white-walled tunnel. She was beginning to realize that Boone had been right; she had no business in such a remote area with darkness approaching in a snowstorm.

A blast of wind raced through the trees, swirling the flakes and vibrating against the car. Her heart began hammering with rapid, jerky beats. Quickly she stifled the nervous impulse that made her toe press more firmly against the accelerator. The road was packed with snow; she couldn't drive any faster or she would lose control of her car and drive into a snowbank. On such a desolate road, she might be out all night.

Suddenly she rounded the last curve. In the semi-darkness the mansion she was to show loomed from out of the trees. It was boldly modern. Normally she would have marveled at the beautiful simplicity of its design and how wondrously it blended with its setting. But not tonight. The wind whistled through the trees, shaking snow loose from the heavily laden branches and swirling it and fluffing it into such dense clouds that Leslie could scarcely see.

Squinting, her eyes straining, she peered at the road. No car tracks marred the smooth whiteness of the snowy road. Nor was any car parked in front, which meant that her client was not here yet. Where was he? she asked herself nervously. Was he going to stand her up?

Fumbling in her purse for the keys to the house, she alighted from her car and made her way carefully up the icy sidewalk. She clutched her silvery fur close around her cheeks and body to keep out the intense frigid gusts of air and snow.

Where was her client? She felt so terribly alone all by herself. Why hadn't she listened to Boone? He'd known what he was talking about, and she'd been so stubbornly set on doing as she'd planned that she'd ignored the wisdom of his advice.

Fleetingly she wondered if she should drive on back to town without even waiting for her client. But she instantly decided that since she was already here, it wouldn't hurt to wait a few more minutes. Suddenly her feet slid on the glassy surface and she almost fell. Gasping, she drew a long, deep breath and decided she must be more careful.

Her body shook violently from the cold, and she'd only been out in it less than a minute. Why hadn't she worn something warmer? But when she'd dressed this morning she hadn't realized it would turn so much colder, nor had she expected to be out like this.

She brushed the crusts of ice from the doorknob. Shaking fingers unlocked the door, and she let herself inside. For one long moment she leaned heavily against the door.

The house was as cold and silent as a vast tomb. At least she was out of the wind, but as she stood shivering beside the door, she realized the temperature inside the house was below freezing. The electricity was turned off, and the house was eerie and uninviting.

Leslie went to a window and looked out, hoping to see the headlights of her client's car. But outside all was darkness, and furious flurries of snow were blowing and drifting. Snow lay a foot deep on the window sill, almost obscuring her view. Snowflakes angrily lashed the window panes, bouncing off and flying away. Wind whipped around the house, and somewhere a loose board banged against a wall.

What was she going to do? How long should she wait? Nervously she chewed on a mittened hand and then decided.

The storm seemed to be growing stronger. If her client wasn't coming, then her best bet was to go on and head down the mountain before it grew any later. She had hoped he would come and that she would be able to trail him down the road. But with every minute that passed it was darkening, and she felt that if he were going to come he would have done so by now.

An explosion—a sound like the mountain itself ripping apart—jarred the house. Then Leslie heard a distant rumbling. She stood very still, as alert as a frightened wild thing as she peered out the window and listened, wondering what had made that noise.

Outside all was as it had been—darkness and thickly falling snow. But the strange thunderous sound had increased her anxiety, and she decided she'd leave at once before anything else happened.

Hastily she pulled the door closed. She was so upset that she didn't realize she hadn't locked it. Then she picked her way across the icy walk through snow —a foot and a half deep by now—to her car. Her ankles felt frozen by the time she slipped inside her car.

Starting the engine, she carefully turned the car around and headed back down the twisting road.

Leslie's emerald eyes widened as she leaned forward

over the steering wheel, struggling to see through the blinding whiteness. It was almost impossible.

Suddenly ahead of her she saw snow piled deeply across the road and fallen trees scattered about as though they were matches that had tumbled haphazardly out of their box.

The road was blocked! She remembered the explosion she'd heard and suddenly knew that it had been an avalanche. For a long moment, she stared as though paralyzed at the mass of trees and snow and ice the size of box cars that cut off the road.

If she'd left for Winter Park any sooner, she would have been crushed. . . . Her face was white with tension; her heart was pounding fiercely.

Instead of relief she felt terror; there was no way back to Winter Park but down that road. She was trapped!

Her expression was bleak and lost. Without the proper clothes and food she would surely freeze to death. She knew nothing about survival in the snow.

Her mind raced, and thinking of the house she'd left behind, she decided that it was probably well insulated and offered more protection from the elements than her car. She would go back there and wait. And hope. . . .

A vision of Karen, her blue eyes brilliant with their customary excitement, her thick chestnut curls framing the delicate beauty of her angelic face, her bright smile. . . . Then instantly the dearly beloved dark visage of Boone sprang into her mind, and Leslie had to fight back tears. She wanted to be with them so desperately.

Fear that she would never see the two people she loved most in all the world was a savage emotion that made her feel close to hysteria. This couldn't be happening! It was a nightmare and she was going to wake up!

But it was no nightmare. It was reality turned into a nightmare, and she had to get a grip on herself if she were going to survive. Her whole body was shaking with fright.

At last she managed to force herself to calm down. Cautiously she attempted to turn the car around, but to her horror she backed too far into the drifts along the side of the road, and the back tires began to spin helplessly. She was hopelessly stuck.

This had happened to her before when driving in the snow around Winter Park, but always there had been someone nearby to help push her out. Now there was no one.

Shifting to neutral, she got out of the car and tried to push, but she was not strong enough. The car didn't budge, even when she was breathless from her exertions.

The mountain trembled beneath her feet, and Leslie held her breath. Another avalanche! Oh, dear God . . . She prayed silently that she would not be swept down the mountain like another piece of rubble.

She heard a furious rumbling and panicking, she began to run down the road back toward the house. Her lungs felt clogged, and she was gasping for breath. But still she ran. Snow was drifting like shallow waves over the road; snow, knee deep, was sliding over the road bed and down the side of the mountain.

She was caught in the fringe of the avalanche. But she struggled against the tide of powdery cold swirling up to her knees; she struggled against her own exhaustion.

She fell down several times, cutting her legs on the icy road and ripping her nylon hose. But each time she got up and forced herself to walk back toward the house. Her feet and legs felt numb. Her breaths came in harsh burning gasps. Every part of her felt frozen, but she ignored her pain and fear. She was intent on one thing only—getting back to the house.

Finally the snow stopped moving. It lay across the road in deep drifts, but she was able to stumble through it more easily until finally she reached the house.

Fortunately she hadn't driven too far down the road. Wearily she dragged herself up to the door, and when she pushed it, it opened. She practically fell inside.

Stepping into the kitchen she opened the pantry. It was a small airless room, but because it was so tiny perhaps her body heat—if she still had any—would warm it. Taking off her coat, she pulled the door until it was almost shut and huddled beneath her soft fur, rubbing her frozen legs and forcing her toes to move in a vain attempt to warm herself.

Oh, please, please let someone find her before . . . it was too late.

Waves of darkness seemed to curl over her, and she fought desperately to stay conscious. Never had she felt so tired, as though she wanted to sink into the deepest of sleeps.

"Boone . . . Boone." She said his name over and over again in a breathless sigh of despair. He would come for her. He had to.

It seemed that she lay in the cold dark airless space for hours. Her muscles were cramped, her throat dry, her legs cut and bleeding. She drifted in and out of consciousness.

Sometime during the night she thought a light flashed, but when she opened the pantry door and looked out, the house was shrouded in darkness. Once more she fell asleep, awakening again a short time later because of a faint purring sound.

Terror brought her instantly awake. Was it another avalanche? But as she strained to hear, the only sounds were the faint stirrings of the wind. She realized the intensity of the storm had lessened.

Every part of her ached with cold, and she stretched beneath her fur coat. Somewhere outside she heard scraping sounds as though someone were tramping through the snow. A man's voice. . . . Her name. . . . Leslie's heart leapt with excitement before she wondered dismally if she were hallucinating.

Something heavy thudded against the house. The front door was thrown open, and the most wonderful sound Leslie had ever heard filled the house—Boone's voice calling her name.

"Leslie!" The deep sound echoed through the empty house.

"Boone . . . over here." Her own voice was weak and faint. When she tried to stand up, a dizzying nauseous feeling swept through her and she collapsed, her limp body spilling onto the cold tile floor of the kitchen.

When her lashes fluttered open a minute later she was wrapped in Boone's arms, thick blankets bundled over her legs and body. A propane lamp gleamed from the kitchen cabinet.

Boone's dark face was gentle as he gazed down at her. A cut above his dark eyebrow was open and oozed a faint trail of blood down the side of his face.

She was struggling to sit upright, and he helped her. Relief that he was really here, that he'd come in time

162

fought against her rising hysteria. She'd been truly terrified. Suddenly she began to shake, and Boone cradled her against the broad warmth of his chest. It felt so good—his holding her close. Never had any sensation been more comforting. Her head rested against his shoulder; her golden hair streamed over his arms.

She felt his fingers smoothing back her tangled hair, his touch as gentle as a caress. She clung to him and sobbed quietly, feeling that if he ever let go of her she'd never feel safe again. Tears spilled over her long lashes, staining her cheeks with mascara. She wondered if she'd ever be able to stop crying.

Only vaguely was she aware of him gently drying her tears on a monogrammed handkerchief he pulled from his coat pocket, of him lifting her to her feet. He tucked her silver fur coat more closely around her shoulders. Then he folded his arms protectively around her.

"Leslie, are you all right?" His strong brown hand cupped her chin gently. "I saw your car upside down on the side of the mountain."

"I—I had gotten out of it . . . in time. . . ." Her voice broke, and she blinked against a new surge of tears. She felt shattered inside.

"Thank God," he murmured, staring deeply into her eyes as though she were very precious to him. "If anything had happened to you . . . I don't think I would have ever forgiven myself." He paused. "I'm going to fly you home."

"Fly . . ."

"I got the federal rangers to fly me up here in their helicopter."

"Oh, Boone, you're hurt." A sob caught in her throat

at the sight of his bruised and bleeding hands. With her fingertips she wiped at the blood smeared on his cheek. "What happened?"

"It's nothing. Cut myself jumping out of the helicopter."

"And it's my fault. If I'd listened to you in the first place . . ."

"Hush. . . . It's okay." His hand wrapped around her fingers that were lightly brushing his cheek. "I understand why you did what you did. You couldn't have known what would happen."

He was being so infinitely gentle, so completely kind. Her heart was filled with love and gratitude as she smiled weakly up at him.

Leaning heavily on his arm, Leslie was guided outside into the brisk cold then down the road to a clearing where the helicopter hovered like a giant dark bumblebee.

Boone lifted Leslie into the waiting arms of one of the rangers and then jumped inside the helicopter himself. The pilot rose abruptly at a sharp angle and flew toward Winter Park.

The warmth from the heater blasted around Leslie, but in spite of that she snuggled against Boone.

Above the vibration and noise of the helicopter Leslie yelled, "I kept thinking my client would show up. But he never did. I wonder what happened to him?"

"He called right after you left," Boone said. "I was still in the office, and I took his call. When he said he'd been out and you couldn't have reached him, I wondered if you might not come on up to the house. I decided I'd better check."

"I'm glad you did," she murmured gratefully. "I should have listened to you."

"In the future I'll expect you to obey me unconditionally," he teased, patting her hair. "When I tried to drive up I found the road was blocked, so I went back to Winter Park and talked Kelly here into risking his neck and flying me up here."

Kelly winked over his shoulder and then turned all his attention back to flying the helicopter.

A comfortable silence lapsed between Boone and Leslie. Leslie felt that she was at last thawing out. She could feel her toes tingling. Her teeth were no longer chattering.

As she lay in Boone's arms, she reflected that only in Boone's presence could she feel this snug, wonderful sense of security.

Half an hour later when he had escorted her safely inside her condominium they began to talk again.

"Where's Karen?" he asked. "Gini's?"

"Yes." Leslie sank wearily onto the couch, nervous exhaustion sweeping her. She didn't feel up to facing her lively child just yet.

"That's a good place for her for the time being," Boone said, sensing how she felt. "I'll give Gini a call and explain."

"Would you?" she asked gratefully. "I–I don't feel up to any . . . explanations . . . tonight."

He made the call and arranged for Karen to stay overnight with Gini. Then he strode to the bar and poured two glasses of Scotch over ice. Returning to Leslie's side, Boone handed her a glass and then lifted his own, swirled the liquid and ice cubes in one quick motion, lifted it to his lips, and drained it.

When she sipped hers slowly, the strong liquor scalded her throat. Sputtering, she would have set the glass on the table beside the couch, but Boone's brown hand arrested hers. A faint, warming tingle shivered through her at his touch.

"Drink it," he commanded. "All of it. It will not only warm you up but it'll help you to relax."

"I haven't eaten. I–I'm not used to such a strong drink," she protested. "It makes me feel . . . funny."

His handsome face was set in hard, stubborn lines. "Drink it."

Only when she obediently brought the glass to the pouting curve of her lips once more did the tension drain from his hard features. She drank almost all of it before she set the glass down and coughed. "I need some water," she choked, starting to rise. "I really do."

"Stay where you are. I'll get it."

Gratefully she reached for the glass of tap water he brought her from the kitchen. When she'd finished drinking it, he knelt down in front of her.

His hands separated the edges of her fur coat, and she felt the warmth of his touch move slowly over her as though he were examining her like a doctor. Slowly his hands explored downward over her legs, her feet and toes.

Involuntarily she cringed away from him as his hands touched a bruised place on her bare leg. "Don't . . . Boone," she murmured, trying to push his hands away. "Please . . ." A bright flush suffused her cheeks at the intimacy of his gesture.

"Leslie, I want to see if you're hurt," he insisted. His deep voice was gentle with concern and yet firm.

"I–I'm all right," she said. "Really. . . . You don't have to . . ." A strange shyness was sweeping her, a ridiculous modesty, and she clutched her coat together and tried to curl her legs underneath her.

"If you won't let me, I'll have to call Dr. Rome."

"No. . . . I don't need a doctor. I'll be all right. I've been through enough tonight."

"Leslie, I know you're tired, but I have no intention of leaving you tonight without either examining you myself or calling Dr. Rome. Exposure can have very serious consequences. Frostbite . . ."

"Boone . . ."

"You're not going to change my mind," he stated emphatically. His steadfast black gaze held her own, and she knew that he meant what he said.

When she sat defiantly before him for a long moment, Boone shifted his weight to get up, and she knew that he intended to call Dr. Rome.

There was absolutely no point in calling the doctor out in the middle of the night. Instantly she made up her mind. "Wait," she whispered as she reached hesitantly for his hands and led them slowly back to her body. "All right."

His eyes glowed like dark fires as he registered her meaning. A tender smile curved the harsh line of his mouth as he looked down at her. She placed his hands on the bare curve of her legs. The intimacy of his touch caused a strange warm current to ripple through her that wasn't at all unpleasant.

"I'll try not to hurt you, Leslie." His low voice was oddly rough, his expression gentle.

167

He removed her coat so that it slipped over her shoulders. He carefully stripped away her torn stockings and shoes. Skillfully his hands moved over her, and when she moaned slightly with pain he asked her all the appropriate questions and listened for her answers.

She remembered that he'd once studied to be a doctor and that he'd had to drop out of medical school because of his wife. Boone's concern for her was obvious in every movement, in every question that he asked. In that moment Leslie realized what a good doctor he would have been and what a shame it was that he hadn't been able to continue his studies. His heart had been in medicine, not real estate.

Abruptly she thought of Tim and how important his own medical career had been to him. Had he been unable to complete his training to be a doctor, he would never had made the successful adjustment to another career that Boone had made. Boone had an inner strength, a depth of character that most of the men she'd known had lacked.

"I think you're all right—other than a few bruises and surface cuts," he said at last, interrupting her thoughts. "Take a nice long bath and relax. . . . But if you have any pain tonight I want you to promise me you'll call Dr. Rome. And I want you to go in and see him tomorrow."

"Okay, I will."

"Then, if you're settled for the night, I'll be going."

He was rising to his feet; he towered over her like a magnificent dark giant. She realized with a frightened start that he was leaving.

"Boone . . ." Her voice was a tiny quavering sound that reached out and touched him.

He was slipping his sheepskin coat over his broad

shoulders. "Ummm," he replied absently, looking down at her.

"Boone, I—I'm scared. I don't want you to go."

The black fire of his gaze went over her quizzically, and she felt warmed through by the tenderness of his expression. Quickly she jumped to her feet and reached for one of his hands. The sudden movement caused her coat to slide the rest of the way down her shoulders so that she stood before him with her clinging sweater revealing the shape of her breasts. Her tattered skirt hung about her legs in strips. But as her hand made contact with his, she flushed as he looked down at her, desire suddenly scrawled across his handsome features.

Boone forced himself to look away as though the sight of her semi-clad body disturbed him uncontrollably. Even though he wasn't looking at her, Leslie realized that he was keenly aware of her beauty, of her golden hair falling softly over her breasts and shoulders, of the delicate golden-toned loveliness of her flesh, of her diminutive femininity. She roused him, and he sought to reject this reality.

"I need to talk to Kelly," he said grimly, pulling the keys to his truck from his pocket. "You're safe now. There's no reason for me to stay." When she clung to his hand stubbornly, he said, "I'll call you later . . . and make sure you're all right."

He stepped toward the door, but she held onto his hand, pulling him back.

"Please, stay with me . . . tonight," she pleaded. Then she wrapped her arms around him tightly as though to bodily prevent him from leaving. Her breasts were crushed against the massive heat of his chest, her lovely face was tilted upward so that she could stare deeply into his eyes. "Please . . . don't go. . . . I know it sounds stupid, but I need you. I was so afraid up there . . . all alone. I don't want to be alone tonight."

She was acutely aware of everywhere that his body touched hers. She felt his muscles stiffen, and when he spoke his voice was harsh. "Leslie, do you have any idea what you're doing to me? You're touching me . . . so that I can feel the heat of you, your softness against me. . . . You want me to spend the night . . . to keep you company and make you feel safe. But I don't know if I can. I know what you went through up there on the mountain, and in spite of that, I want you. But you're in no condition . . ."

His words trailed off, yet in the pregnant silence that lapsed between them she was aware of an intense emotional tension growing between them.

"I don't blame you for how you feel," she said softly. "If you'll only stay—I'll leave you alone. I'll get dressed in something that buttons up to my chin, and I won't get any nearer than across the room to you."

His lips twisted sardonically. "Perhaps that's carrying things a bit far," he mused dryly. "If you'd just put some clothes on I'd probably be able to put the lid on those . . . er . . . predatory masculine instincts you so aptly accused me of understanding earlier. Here, wrap up in your coat for starters."

He reached down and pulled her coat over her slim shoulders so that she was completely swathed in silver fur.

"I know that we're not interested in being . . . personally involved with each other . . . any longer," she murmured shyly. "And I'm not expecting that. I don't even want it. I just want you to stay tonight. You can sleep in the guest bedroom. I won't come near you."

An odd light flickered in the depths of his black eyes, and for a minute she wondered if she'd thoughtlessly said the wrong thing and hurt him. Then his face was a smooth dark mask once more, his taut expression unreadable. She thought she must have imagined that quick look of hurt.

He heard the desperation in her voice; he sensed her irrational terror. Understanding the reason behind her fear, he couldn't stop himself from wanting to help her.

"All right. You talked me into it." There was a smile in his deep voice. Her own face was wreathed in radiant happiness as she looked up at him.

"It's a good thing I wasn't born a woman," he said, attempting a lightness as he shrugged out of his coat again and tossed it onto the chair. His keys jingled faintly as he set them on the coffee table. "Because I never have had the strength of character to say no even when I know I should to a woman as beautiful as you."

11

Although Boone spent the rest of the night with her, even in her small condominium, he managed to avoid having personal contact with her. First he insisted that she go back to her room and take a long bath.

When she came out of her bath dressed in her thick emerald corduroy robe, he was sitting at the dining room table, his brief case open and files scattered about. He looked up disinterestedly from his papers, saying pleasantly, "I hope I won't be in your way here. I had these contracts and blueprints in my truck because I was planning to work late at home. Since it's late and I'm going to spend the night, I might as well get down to work here."

"No. . . . You won't be in my way," she replied weakly, fighting back a twinge of disappointment that he so obviously preferred working to talking with her.

He bent his black head and began scribbling something rapidly on several sheets of paper. She realized he'd completely forgotten she was there.

Slowly she moved into the kitchen and began rummaging furiously through her pantry. Only when he glanced up impatiently in her direction did she stop and realize she was acting like a child. She wanted him to pay attention to her, and he clearly had no intention of doing so. She bit a nail in frustration and forced herself to move more quietly.

Taking a tray filled with crackers and cheeses into the dining room, she set it beside him. "I thought you might be hungry," she offered.

"Why thank you, Leslie," he replied absently, never looking up from his work. "But you don't need to worry about me. I can find whatever I need. You go on to bed and get some sleep. I'll probably be at this the rest of the night."

Never had she felt so completely rejected. But what had she thought would happen? He hadn't wanted to stay with her. He'd done so only because she'd insisted. Suddenly she saw with a new clarity that although he found her physically attractive, he was totally indifferent to her as a person. He no longer wanted any personal involvement with her.

He'd rescued her as he would have saved any woman in the same situation. She meant nothing special to him other than the fact that she was a valuable employee. He'd told her that himself that afternoon in his office. What was it going to take before she realized that their relationship was over?

Nothing else, she vowed silently as she pressed out the light beneath the Chinese silk lampshade beside her bed.

"Nothing." Faintly she murmured the word. He was lost to her . . . forever. . . . Perhaps he always had been. He had said from the beginning that he wanted no involvement with any woman, that he'd been badly burned in the past. He hadn't been able to believe that her feelings for him were deep, that her going out with Tim had meant nothing. And if he couldn't trust her, if they couldn't communicate, their relationship never had had a chance. If only . . .

Darkness swirled around her. The effects of the double Scotch never had worn off. The emotional trauma she'd endured had exhausted her more than she realized. And because she knew that Boone was in the other room, and that she was utterly safe, she fell into a deep and soundless sleep.

The events of the day affected her even in her sleep. Several hours later she awoke in the pitch blackness of her bedroom. She was cold with sweat, and she sobbed incoherently.

She was back at Hunter's Creek again in the dark, swirling snowstorm. Again she was plunging through snow, only with every step the snow seemed to grow deeper, and she was sinking into it as though it were an icy quick sand, sucking her under and down the mountain. The harder she fought, the deeper she sank. She was aware of her complete helplessness. Her heart was near bursting as it pounded against her ribcage. Then she began screaming—that terrible soundless scream of nightmares. Then her own voice, high-pitched and desperate, broke through the black silence.

"Help! Oh, please . . . please help . . . Boone!"

Suddenly Boone was leaning over her, and without a word he drew her into his arms as though she were a child and held her close against his hard muscular chest, his low voice soothing away her fears until her sobbing ceased.

"Oh, Boone, I was back at Hunter's Creek. In the storm. I . . . I was sinking into the snow. I–it was like drowning . . . I–I . . ."

"Hush, darling," he murmured. His warm breath quivered over her bare flesh, scalding her into a pleasant awareness of him. "It was only a dream."

"But it seemed so real."

"You're safe now. Nothing like that will ever happen to you again."

He pulled her onto his lap and cradled her gently against him for a long while. One of his hands stroked through the tumbling masses of her hair. The other gently rubbed the bare flesh of her back as he pressed her close against himself. Her face rested against the prickly black hair covering his bare chest, and she could hear the quick, uneven pounding of his heart.

Slowly new sensations stirred through her. The steady motion of his hand through her hair sent a fiery tingle of shock waves through her. She was intently aware of the hard pressure of his thighs against her own. It had been so long since he'd made love to her, and she loved him so desperately that suddenly, unexpectedly, she wanted him beyond reason. She was a woman with a woman's needs. And he was the man she loved.

Because she was still drowsy with sleep she was no longer so aware of the barriers that separated them. Forgotten for the moment was the fact that Boone had rejected her. She wanted him, and the hard pressure of his body told her that he wanted her.

She wasn't exactly sure when or how it happened, but

Boone's embrace changed from being comforting to being sexual. His hands moved languorously over her with their sure, expert knowledge of how to awaken her desire. Her pulse was racing, and she was aware that his raced no less intensely.

Her filmy nightgown was tangled about her creamy thighs. The sheet he'd wrapped around himself when he'd heard her screams had fallen away, and she could no longer ignore the fact that he was naked beneath it. The length of his hot bronzed flesh was crushed tightly against her female form, and when her curves were molded to the hard contours of his masculinity, Boone's low groan of arousal vibrated thrillingly through her.

With a complete and shattering mastery his lips sought hers, claiming them in a fiercely passionate kiss. Her lips parted for the intimate invasion of his tongue. She felt his hands moving over her, seeking out the softness of her breasts, as though he wanted and needed to feel her flesh completely against his own. Her filmy nightgown prevented his body from having total contact with her. And the raw urgency of his passion drove him to rip at the gauzy fabric. Leslie made a feeble attempt to stop him, but her own passion swept her away. And Boone's strong hands shredded her nightgown.

More of her bare flesh touched his, and she felt hotly alive, flaming with desire. He shifted her in his arms so that she lay beneath him, so that his teak-brown torso lay on top of her soft breasts, so that her hips fitted his. His lips moved from her mouth, downward over her throat, their teasing and nibbling wreaking erotic havoc with her senses.

In the burning darkness she was aware only of him,

only of the bruising, demanding feel of his mouth on her bare skin, of his aroused body crushed tightly to hers.

As he intimately explored her voluptuous curves with his mouth and tongue and hands, she lay against the soft mattress lost in the thick swirling passion of his embrace.

She loved him, and she didn't care about anything in all the world except being with him. This moment of supreme, glorious, sensuality obliterated everything except her intense awareness of the present and the man who made love to her.

He drew her deeper and deeper into a dark world of passion where she experienced wild thrilling feelings such as she had never known before—blinding happiness, exquisite terror, flaming excitement. She surrendered herself completely to this man who took her with bruising force, mastering her, dominating her, loving her with devastating totality. In the thick enveloping darkness she was aware only of hard arms circling her, of the intense heat of his body everywhere his touched hers, of the hot, traitorous need flooding through her veins.

For one intensely shattering moment they merged completely—body and soul. When he would have withdrawn from her, she clung to him, weeping soundlessly, her tears falling onto his chest and dampening his hot flesh. Finally she fell asleep, wrapped in the hard, protective warmth of his arms.

A pattern of bright sunlight played against the white curtain in Leslie's bedroom the next morning when she yawned widely, awakening.

"Boone," she murmured drowsily, reaching across the bed for him. Her long lashes fluttered indolently and she opened her eyes.

An odd little pain stabbed her. He was gone, and had it not been for the shredded nightgown on the floor and the rumpled pillow on the other side of the bed, she would never have been sure the night of passion she was remembering was not a wild figment of her imagination. As her green gaze focused on the filmy strips of her nightgown on the beige carpet, she blushed deep crimson. Last night the fierceness of his desire had been beyond anything in her experience, and her own need had risen to match his.

She lay contentedly back against her pillow, a tiny smile playing with the edges of her mouth as she remembered the rapturous ecstasy of her surrender to the only man she could ever love.

Boone loved her! He had said it in that final moment when they had been joined together. No matter what had ever been between them in the past, she was sure that she meant more to him than he'd ever been willing to admit. A man didn't lie . . . at a time like that . . . did he?

Yet later when he called that morning, she wondered.

His crisp voice was emotionally remote, and she clutched the receiver more tightly, a strange chill shivering through her.

"Leslie, Kelly and another federal ranger want to talk to you. I'll drive you to his office and then to see Dr. Rome in an hour . . . if you can be ready," he stated curtly.

There was not one word of endearment for her, no mention of last night and that it had meant anything special to him. Suddenly she was shaking uncontrollably because of his coldness. Something was dreadfully wrong!

"Boone . . . last night," she began unsteadily, "when you came to my room . . . I thought . . ."

Savagely he cut her off. "Last night was a mistake," he said coldly. "I take full responsibility for what happened, and I'm sorry."

"But Boone . . ."

"I knew that I had no business staying overnight with you. Believe me, I regret what happened as deeply as you do."

Leslie's heart pounded dully. Each pulsebeat produced a tiny constricting pain. He continued talking, but she scarcely listened.

He didn't love her! He was sorry for what had happened between them! It was all too obvious he wanted no involvement with her! And she'd thought, she'd truly believed that he loved her! What a love-sick fool she was—grasping at straws, hoping against hope that he cared something for her.

"Leslie, I want you to take that job in Vail," he was saying, still in that same cold tone that was freezing her emotions. "I think it's for the best. In fact I'll drive you over there tomorrow myself so you can look into it. I won't hold you to your contract with me if you want out, and I'll pay your moving expenses."

Oh, Boone, no, no, no! she wanted to cry out, but pride kept her silent. He didn't want her; he wanted her gone. She'd tried everything she could think of to save their relationship, and she realized with awful finality that it was time to give up. But last night and the new closeness she felt for him made this more difficult than ever for her to bear. She gasped at the intensity of sheer, raw, aching sensation that ripped brutally through her.

"Thank you, Boone, for everything," she heard herself mouth mechanically. "I appreciate all that you're doing. You couldn't be more generous."

The next two weeks passed in a dismal blur. Boone had helped her buy a new car and driven her to Vail as he'd offered, and when he'd heard the terms of the new job offer, he insisted that she take it. In no way could he have been kinder or more helpful.

But every act of kindness, every way that he helped her only proved to Leslie how deeply anxious he was to be rid of her. She realized that she no longer had any choice about leaving. If he were this desperate to have her gone, she must go. If she loved him at all, she would do as he wanted and leave him.

Leslie was snapping the last of her suitcases shut. Boxes, packed to the brim, teetered in precarious stacks about the living room. The movers wouldn't be arriving for several days, but she was leaving today in her car for Vail. All she had left to do now was pick up Karen at school. . . .

For a long moment her eyes wandered around the familiar room. A hot tear pricked from behind her lashes but didn't fall as she stared at the place in front of the fireplace where Boone had first made love to her.

She hadn't lived in Winter Park very long, but she had a heart full of memories that would have to last her a lifetime. Well, there was no point in dwelling on them now. She would never be able to leave if she did.

Slowly she stooped to pick up the leather handles of her purse. Then she headed toward the front door to go down to the garage and finish loading her car.

Just as she was about to swing the door open, a brisk knock sounded from the other side. Then the doorbell buzzed once and then again.

She flung open the door, and a little gasp of amazement and joy escaped her lips as her eyes met Boone's black gaze. He looked haggard and gaunt. He hadn't shaved, and his broad shoulders drooped slightly as though he were either despondent or exhausted. But as always, to her he was the most handsome of men, the most welcome sight in all the world.

"Boone." There was a strange lilting sound in her husky voice as she welcomed him; she'd thought she would never see him again. Her beautiful face was illuminated with joy as she stared up at him.

His own expression was utterly bleak. He looked like a man who'd lost whatever it was he prized most in life, a man who'd reached the bottom of despair.

Reading his emotion, she cried out, suddenly stricken with concern. "Boone, what is it? What's wrong?"

Her slender hand reached out and seized his, and he drew back as if burned. She was reminded of his distaste for her, and yet if something were wrong, if he needed help. . . . She had to know if there was some way she could help him.

"Boone, why did you come over? Tell me!"

"I . . . I came by to tell you goodbye," he said slowly. "I wanted to see if you had anything heavy to lift . . . if you needed any help. . . ."

So he'd only come by to help her leave—or to make sure that she left.

If only he hadn't, she could have kept her fragile control. But the sight of him, the hot sensation of his hand in hers, was suddenly too much for her. And the tears that hadn't fallen streamed down her cheeks. She sobbed brokenly and hated herself for doing so.

"You shouldn't have come by," she cried out desperately, wrenching her hand free from his. "I didn't want you to. Why couldn't you just let me go?"

"Leslie . . ." His deep voice was hoarse with passion and pain.

Then his hard strong arms were circling her in a vain attempt to comfort her. For a fraction of a second she melted in his arms, but then she realized what was happening to her. She balled her hands into fists and pounded at his broad chest frantically. She couldn't bear for him to hold her when he felt nothing for her.

"Let me go, Boone. Don't you know what you do to me when you hold me? Don't you understand that it's torture—your touching me?"

Her quivering voice seemed to pierce him like a quick, savage blade, and abruptly he let her go. Shaking, she collapsed against the chair. To her surprise she saw that his own dark face was ashen as though he were suffering as intensely as she.

"I'm sorry, Leslie, but I had to see you again—one last time."

The terrible finality in his ragged tone slashed through her, and she sagged with defeat.

Nothing had changed between them. He didn't care. He never would.

12

⬥⬥⬥⬥⬥⬥⬥⬥⬥

I wouldn't have come, Leslie, if I'd known how much it would upset you. But I want you to know that I don't blame you for feeling the way you do. I've hated myself, despised myself for what I did to you."

"What you did to me?" she repeated quietly. The anguished pain in his low voice caught at a corner of her heart. Never had she felt more vulnerable to his virile appeal. She didn't understand what he was driving at.

"In spite of what happened . . . two weeks ago . . . when I spent the night here, I never meant to hurt you. My God. . . . You'd been hurt—nearly killed up at Hunter's Creek that evening. And then that very same night I ripped your nightgown to shreds and forced myself on you . . . after you'd told me you didn't ever want to be personally involved with me again. I know you only let me make love to you because I'd rescued you, and you felt grateful."

She stared wonderingly up at him. Was that really what he had believed? Had he really been so deeply stricken with guilt because he thought he'd hurt her? She saw the deep lines of suffering etched into his face, and suddenly she knew that he had.

"You didn't hurt me, Boone," she began very softly, her eyes shining with her love for him. New hope fluttered in her chest as her heart began to beat jerkily. "Not that night . . . not ever. I wanted you as much as you wanted me."

There was disbelief in his swift dark glance that met her own shimmering one.

"Boone, I mean what I'm saying. You've always thought you understood me, even when you didn't. But it's very important to me that you know you have nothing to feel guilty about for that night. That—well, it was the most beautiful experience in my life," she admitted brokenly. "The only way you hurt me is that after being with you again, after thinking that we'd found each other again, I can hardly bear to leave you, even though I know it's for the best."

His black eyes gleamed fiercely as he stared with burning intensity at her exquisite features. "It's for the best. . . . Whose best?"

"Because it's what you want," she whispered.

"The hell it is," he muttered fiercely, dragging her into the hard force of his arms and holding her closely against himself for a wondrously long moment.

"Boone, what are you saying. I–I don't understand."

Unexpected contact with his masculine body made her tremble slightly.

"I want you back, Leslie." His hand moved through her hair in a slow, caressing motion. "If you really meant what you said, I want you back. But I don't want to force myself on you. The only reason I was helping you move was because I thought you wanted to go—to get away from me. I didn't want to stand in your way."

"Oh, Boone, I can't believe it."

"I love you, Leslie," he murmured huskily, his hot breath stirring the silken tendrils at her temple. "I think I have from the moment I saw you that day at the ski slope. You were beautiful like Marnie, and yet there was a sweetness, a softness to you that she never had. I'd loved her for so long, or at least I thought I did. And then I hated her when I found out what she was really like. I blamed myself for her death because there was a part of me that had wanted her dead."

"Are you sure that it's me you want . . . and not her?" Leslie whispered anxiously, remembering Tess's words on the mountain.

"The minute I saw you I was struck with the resemblance between you and her. My feelings for Marnie were powerful even after she died. I thought her beautiful, I wanted her physically, and yet she used her power over me. She never loved me. I'd wanted to be a doctor all my life, but when I got her pregnant, I dropped out of medical school and married her because she mattered more to me than anything else. Years later I found out that she aborted our child deliberately. I couldn't forgive her for that. She began drinking. There were other men, but still my feelings for her ran so deep I couldn't divorce her. We had a terrible quarrel the night she died. She was drunk, and I was so angry I let her go out anyway. . . . When she died . . . I blamed myself."

"It wasn't your fault," Leslie said softly, seeking to comfort him.

"Then I met you. I think I saw almost at once that your resemblance to Marnie was only superficial. But I wouldn't trust my instincts. You had that same power over me that she had had, only it was even more intense. When I found out Mother had deliberately hired you, I was convinced for a while you were as conniving as Marnie was. Then when I was around you on a day-to-day basis, I was sure you weren't. You looked like her, but you weren't like her. Still, I kept remembering what she'd done, how she'd twisted my life around . . . my very soul. My feelings for you were so intense that I was afraid you would have the same power over me and use it as she had to destroy me. I couldn't trust you because of her. Even when I wanted to."

"Oh, Boone, if only you'd told me all this sooner. I would have understood. I know what it's like to be hurt by the one person you trust. That's what happened to me when Tim walked out. I think I sensed how deeply you'd been hurt that first day you helped me ski down the mountain."

His black head lowered to her golden one, and his mouth claimed hers in a tenderly fierce kiss that inflamed every sense in her body. She quivered from his touch.

"Why didn't you go back to Tim?" he asked very quietly.

"You big lug," she whispered passionately. Then she smiled tenderly. "Do I have to spell it out for you? Because I loved you . . . and only you. . . . I tried to tell you that I went out with him because of Karen and not because I wanted to. I didn't sleep with him. Since the moment I met you, you've been the only man in my life."

The fierce dark light in his eyes seared her as they searched her soul and saw that she was telling the truth. Then his lips smothered hers again. The hot, moist contact of his possessive mouth sent a wildly glorious fire racing through her veins, and she clung to him, pressing her body against him.

She was breathless when he dragged his lips from hers, and the feeling remained when he lowered his mouth to her earlobe and burned a trail of tingling fire along the sensitive skin of her throat.

Suddenly she felt his great body shaking against hers, and a wild tremor shuddered through her as she realized that he was as aroused as she.

"There's one question I haven't asked you," he said hoarsely against her love-swollen lips.

"What's that, Boone?" she murmured impatiently, wanting him to kiss her and hold her and make love to her more than anything else.

"Will you marry me?"

The deep passion in his voice vibrated through her.

"Oh, Boone . . ." she sighed, blissfully happy. Never had she been so happy. And then when her lips met his again in passionate surrender, she communicated the answer to his question without words.

Vaguely she was aware of him kicking the door shut with his boot. Until that moment she hadn't even realized that it was still open. He lifted her into his arms and strode with her toward the bedroom. Gently he placed her on the bed and lowered himself on top of her.

And as he drew her into the hot swirling world of their desire, she knew that from the first their love was meant to be.

Silhouette Desire
15-Day Trial Offer
A new romance series that explores contemporary relationships in exciting detail

Six Silhouette Desire romances, free for 15 days!
We'll send you six new Silhouette Desire romances
to look over for 15 days, absolutely free! If you decide
not to keep the books, return them and owe nothing.

Six books a month, free home delivery. If you like
Silhouette Desire romances as much as we think you
will, keep them and return your payment with the
invoice. Then we will send you six new books every
month to preview, just as soon as they are published.
You pay only for the books you decide to keep, and
you never pay postage and handling.

--- MAIL TODAY ---

**Silhouette Desire, Dept. SDSDJK
120 Brighton Road, Clifton, NJ 07012**

Please send me 6 Silhouette Desire romances to keep for
15 days, absolutely free. I understand I am not obligated
to join the Silhouette Desire Book Club unless I decide
to keep them.

Name_____

Address_____

City_____

State_____ Zip_____

This offer expires July 31, 1983

Silhouette Desire

Coming Next Month

Price of Surrender by Stephanie James

Holt Sinclair thought everything had its price
until he met a woman who couldn't be bought.
Adena West had come to him on business but
Holt was more interested in pleasure. She
entered his corporate jungle to become
passion's prey.

Sweet Serenity by Billie Douglass

When Serena was a child, Tom Reynolds
destroyed her happy life. With Tom's
reappearance all the old hurt returned.
Although he made her tremble with passion,
Serena vowed not to fall beneath his spell.

Gentle Conquest by Kathryn Mallory

When rock star Stuart North agreed to buy and
preserve historic Brogan House, he wanted
gray-eyed Robin Elliot as part of the deal.
What he didn't bargain for was the electricity
between them that burst into a flashfire
of passion.

Silhouette Desire

Coming Next Month

Seduction by Design by Erin St. Claire

From the very beginning Tyler Scott made his intentions clear to Hailey — he intended to be her lover. He radiated a raw masculine power that left Hailey helpless with desire and unable to resist him.

Shadow of Betrayal by Nicole Monet

Diana Moreland tried to hate Joshua Cambridge especially now that he returned to claim his son; the nephew she raised all alone. Desperately she fought to keep the child and her heart — and lost both.

Ask Me No Secrets by Ruth Stewart

The past was behind her, and when Allison looked into Forrest Bennett's coal-black eyes she knew the future held a glowing promise of love. But would he love her still when he penetrated to the secret heart of her passion?

YOU'LL BE SWEPT AWAY
WITH SILHOUETTE DESIRE

$1.75 each

1 ☐ CORPORATE AFFAIR James
2 ☐ LOVE'S SILVER WEB Monet
3 ☐ WISE FOLLY Clay
4 ☐ KISS AND TELL Carey

5 ☐ WHEN LAST WE LOVED Baker
6 ☐ A FRENCHMAN'S KISS Mallory
7 ☐ NOT EVEN FOR LOVE Claire

8 ☐ MAKE NO PROMISES Dee
9 ☐ MOMENT IN TIME Simms
10 ☐ WHENEVER I LOVE YOU Smith

$1.95 each

11 ☐ VELVET TOUCH James
12 ☐ THE COWBOY AND THE LADY Palmer
13 ☐ COME BACK, MY LOVE Wallace
14 ☐ BLANKET OF STARS Valley
15 ☐ SWEET BONDAGE Vernon
16 ☐ DREAM COME TRUE Major
17 ☐ OF PASSION BORN Simms
18 ☐ SECOND HARVEST Ross
19 ☐ LOVER IN PURSUIT James

20 ☐ KING OF DIAMONDS Allison
21 ☐ LOVE IN THE CHINA SEA Baker
22 ☐ BITTERSWEET IN BERN Durant
23 ☐ CONSTANT STRANGER Sunshine
24 ☐ SHARED MOMENTS Baxter
25 ☐ RENAISSANCE MAN James
26 ☐ SEPTEMBER MORNING Palmer
27 ☐ ON WINGS OF NIGHT Conrad
28 ☐ PASSIONATE JOURNEY Lovan

29 ☐ ENCHANTED DESERT Michelle
30 ☐ PAST FORGETTING Lind
31 ☐ RECKLESS PASSION James
32 ☐ YESTERDAY'S DREAMS Clay
33 ☐ PROMISE ME TOMORROW Powers
34 ☐ SNOW SPIRIT Milan
35 ☐ MEANT TO BE Major
36 ☐ FIRES OF MEMORY Summers

SILHOUETTE DESIRE, Department SD/6
1230 Avenue of the Americas
New York, NY 10020

Please send me the books I have checked above. I am enclosing $_____
(please add 50¢ to cover postage and handling. NYS and NYC residents please add
appropriate sales tax.) Send check or money order—no cash or C.O.D.'s please.
Allow six weeks for delivery.

NAME _____

ADDRESS _____

CITY _____ STATE/ZIP _____

Silhouette Desire

Now Available

Reckless Passion by Stephanie James

Dana Bancroft's stockbroker sense told
her that beneath Yale Ransom's well groomed exterior
there lurked a primal force . . . anxiously
waiting to be released.

Yesterday's Dreams by Rita Clay

He said his name was "Mr. Lawrence," but
Candra Bishop soon discovered the truth: he was the
stable boy she had adored in her youth.

Promise Me Tomorrow by Nora Powers

Harris Linton was a charmer, the kind of
man artist Jessie Hampton despised—yet couldn't
resist. She knew she couldn't trust him but desire
overpowered rational thought.

Snow Spirit by Angel Milan

Joda Kerris' passions flared when she discovered that
Egan, the man she had fallen in love with, was a lawyer
hired to sue her and Keystone Mountain Ski Resort!

Meant To Be by Ann Major

Before she knew he was her boss, ravishing
Leslie Grant abandoned herself to Boone Dexter for a
single passionate night. How could she convince
him she loved him?

Fires Of Memory by Ashley Summers

Just when Gia Flynn thought he was safely out
of her life, Adam Kendricks, real-estate tycoon,
returned to San Francisco. This time she would
conquer him once and for all.